D1479234

IMMORTELLE

Catherine McCarthy

To Beet,
my life-long partner, number one beta reader, and permanent shadow.
I couldn't live a day without you.

During the nineteenth century, graveside memorials, known as immortelles, became popular throughout Western Europe. Arrangements of ceramic or beaded flowers, as well as other motifs and trinkets, were displayed beneath glass domes on the graves of those interred as symbols of resurrection and, of course, immortality. As a rule they were not personalised, though the following story imagines them to be...

Welsh terms:

diafol - devil

Suo Gân - lullaby

eira – snow

bach – term of endearment

Mamgu - grandmother

PART ONE

CHAPTER ONE

Elinor

We arrived at the fishing port of Aberporth on the strength of a squall. Rowena's temper was a match for any storm. Hungry and red-faced, she wriggled her balled fists free of the swaddling and shook them toward the heavens. And those lungs! How could one so small reach such a pitch?

The journey from Staffordshire to the west coast of Wales had been long and arduous, unsuited to a newborn baby and a woman already exhausted by grief and betrayal.

The wild Welsh wind seemed in a hurry to see us settled. It gusted at my heels and whipped my hair into my face until I could hardly make out the path beneath my feet. But with Rowena nestled safe and warm in Mamgu's shawl, close to my heart where she belonged, and the prospect of a fresh start for the two of us, I smiled despite the wind.

As we rounded the headland, Rowena spied the village from her woollen peephole and calmed. Round eyes fixed on little rows of white-washed cottages, and she gurgled a sweet story. I swear she knew we would be happy here. And we have been. We have been. Until recently when she suddenly changed.

More than a decade has passed since that day, and she is no longer a babe in arms. When next the hazel dangles its delicate tails among newborn lambs, she will turn twelve. But with age comes secrets. Secrets pocketed in calico aprons that no longer fit. Dark secrets which dare her to slam the door in my face if I probe too deep. Clandestine confidences between her and the bedpost. And if I listened to my heart, I would wrap her tight again in Mamgu's shawl and dare the wind to blow on her.

What ails you, Rowena? At night she tosses and turns, and in the morning rises with crescent moons of gray beneath her eyes to speak of her unrest. There is nothing she need keep from me. No demon I would not slay in her honor. But she has built a wall around her, one which even my maternal hammer cannot break.

At breakfast she stirs her oats round and round the bowl, but the spoon does not reach her lips. Half a year and she will leave school and what will she do then? Assist me in the pottery? She knows the business almost as well as I, for she has watched me work her whole life. The bowl that sits in front of her was crafted with her own hand. Crude flowers, painted by stubby fingers, drip a trail of yellow glaze. The memory of her disappointment as we unloaded the kiln is fresh as a daisy. "It doesn't matter," I told her. "The little yellow carpals drank too much sunshine, that's all." She uncrossed her arms, relaxed a pout, and smiled. When she was a child, I won her around with little effort. That is no longer the case.

Should she decide to apprentice me in the pottery, I will need to teach her to glaze; something I have avoided so far because of the chemicals' toxicity. Not as toxic as her expression, though. "Will you help me after school, Rowena?" I say to break the silence thick as fog. "I'm a little behind with orders."

A glance in my direction, her mouth already forming its refusal, so I play my ace. "I've been thinking...it's about time you learned the glazes. I thought we'd begin with tin."

"Perhaps," she says, which I take to mean yes since the word is followed by three mouthfuls of porridge. I disguise a smile and release my bated breath. I will soften her up, make her forget her troubles for a while, then I will once again ask what worries her.

"How was school?"

She raises her eyes to the heavens and says nothing.

"More of the same?" Maybe I am to blame. Perhaps I should have raised her to accept everything she is told without question.

Her shoulders sag, then she says on a sigh, "Chapter twenty-eight: first book of Samuel." A pause, then she brightens. "Actually, it was rather interesting. Lots of talk of ghosts and mediums. Do you believe in such things, Mam?"

"Which, Rowena? Ghosts or mediums?"

"Either... both, I suppose."

Her hand trembles a little as she stirs the chemicals, eyes flit back and forth toward the glaze recipe, and I wonder if it is because this is the first time I have allowed her to handle the ingredients or because we speak of ghosts. I see her, paused on the brink of womanhood, and wonder how much to divulge. I was raised on Darwin and doubt, not the Bible and baptism, but then Mamgu's methods of raising a child were... *unusual*. "I'm not sure, Rowena." It is a lie because the ghost of my mother visited me on the night of her death. Even though I was four years old, the image is imprinted indelibly. "I like to think death is not the end, that perhaps we meet our loved ones again, but then doesn't everybody?"

"But if you had to say one way or the other?"

She is in the palm of my hand and I do not want to lose her. I smile. "Then yes. I'll go with ghosts. Mediums, I'm not so sure of. You?"

"I believe in both."

"What makes you so certain?"

A shrug, then, "Well, I've seen Mamgu's ghost, and..." Her eyes dart from the glaze bucket to me and back again, gleaning my reaction. When there is none, she continues, "I think there are people who have the gift of contacting the dead."

I hide my surprise, not wanting her to stop. "Perhaps you remember Mamgu from her photograph, Rowena. She died before you were born."

"No: she came to me. She came to tell me everything will be alright." Dark lashes flutter rapidly, the sign of the lie. I have always known from that gesture whether or not she is telling the truth. Does she lie about seeing Mamgu, or does she lie about Mamgu's assurance that everything will be alright?

"Why shouldn't it be? All right, I mean?"

She shakes the excess glaze from the upturned pot, just like I have taught her, but she does not answer my question, instead she fixes her attention on the pot.

"Tell me about Mamgu," she says. "What was she like?"

Changing the subject is a distraction, but I humor her, even though I have spoken of Mamgu many times in the past. "I was four when my mother died, Rowena. Too young to remember her clearly. As you know, Mamgu took me in and raised me as her own. It must have been hard for her, losing her daughter and having to deal with her own grief as well as that of her grandchild.

I suppose I had a somewhat unconventional upbringing. Not because my grandmother raised me, but because of the kind of woman she was." I lean my elbows on the worktop and study Rowena's features. "You take after her, you know. High cheekbones, soulful eyes. Mamgu was kind, but a bit—"

"A bit what?"

"Unusual." I take a deep breath. "She believed in the power of nature. Some called her Pagan. In fact, she worshipped nothing. Belief is not the same as worship, Rowena."

"Like you believe in ghosts, even though you've never seen one?"

I busy myself with stacking the glazed crockery. Should I tell her? "The night my mother died, Rowena." I return to the workbench in order to witness her reaction. "Even at the age of four I understood how sick she was. I have a distant memory of her in the bed, all bones and ragged breath, which frightened me, though I had no concept of death. During the night I woke to see her sitting at the bottom of my bed. She seemed better, happier. Her cheeks flushed pink for the first time in ages. She smiled at me but did not speak." I sense Rowena holding her breath. "The next morning, Mamgu told me she was gone.

"I've not seen a ghost since, not even Mamgu's, despite how close we were." Such talk has captured her interest. I can tell by the way her eyes sparkle. I must try to get her to open up. "And you? With Mamgu? Why do you think she told you everything will be alright?" A shake of the head and a vacant expression warns me not to push too hard.

"Can we go back to the house now? All this talk of death makes me feel ill," she says.

A last ditch attempt. "There is nothing you can't tell me. Nothing I wouldn't do to protect you, no matter how—"

"I don't *know* why she said it." A flick of the hair. A bite of the lip. "Don't spoil things."

We work in silence, tidying away jars of chemicals and wiping down work surfaces. As I rinse the cloth in the bucket, she climbs onto the worktop, just like she did when she was little. The night is cold. Outside, the dark sky twinkles a coded message as she presses her face to the glass. Her breath condenses, and I watch her trace ferns of frost with her finger before she flattens her palm against the surface. I stand close, breathing in the familiar scent of Castile soap and rosemary, before placing my own warm hand on top of hers. Hidden beneath mine but only by a margin. She grows so quick. Our reflections study each other: hers pale, ghost-like, and mine flushed with concern.

"And God?" she says. "Do you believe in God?" She turns to face me, wriggling further along the worktop to break the physical bond.

"I believe there is more to this world than we understand."

"But that's not an answer. God, yes or no." She has always been determined, free-thinking, as I raised her to be.

"Then the answer is no, at least not in the biblical sense. I don't believe some omnipotent being created all this." A wide sweep of the arm. "Nor do I believe any one entity has control over our destiny. Life is what you make it, Rowena. Each of us is responsible for the quality of our own lives."

She watches me through narrowed eyes. Her expression gives no quarter. "Then why do we attend church?"

The answer does not come easy, and when it does, it sounds fake. "We attend church because we belong to this parish, Rowena. I arrived here, remember, with no more than what I could carry, and its people welcomed us with open arms. As far as they were concerned, one of their flock had returned."

"What do you mean? You make it sound as if it's from the Bible."

"I mean this place is our heartland. Mamgu was born and bred here, as was my mother, and people around here remember such things."

She raises her eyes as if it is of little consequence.

"And besides, church is a communal gathering place. Everyone attends." I shrug. My words sound pathetic, but it is true. These people are our family now. "Without these people I would have no business. They are loyal customers as well as friends, remember. Where do you think the food on our table comes from? Charity?" This last comment is harsh, unnecessary, but her sullen expression raises my hackles. "I'm sorry, Rowena. When you are older, you can do as you choose, but for now we attend church because it is expected of us. And remember, attending does not stop you from having your own thoughts and beliefs."

She slides from worktop to floor, a weightless sparrow, and I realize I have achieved very little this evening. Now she knows about the ghost of my mother, but I am no closer to unravelling her worries. Before I can turn down the lamps, she disappears, like some dark-haired pwca, and I am left to trace her footprints in the frost.

CHAPTER TWO

Rowena

There are times when I despise my curious nature. Yet again it has landed me in trouble. Deep down, I blame my mother because she raised me to question things and to make my own choices. My anger toward her is one reason I keep things secret, but not the only reason. If I am honest, she has become my scapegoat.

The first memory I have of her allowing me to learn from my mistakes is an old one. We were at the beach. I must have been around the age of five because I seem to remember the threat of starting school licking at my feet as the tide rolled in. As much as Mam tried to make school sound exciting, I knew I would hate it. It would mean losing the magic of the world we had created together at the beach and in the potter's shed.

On the shore, nestled among a clump of seaweed, I found a strange object: black, roughly rectangular in shape with curly tendrils at one end, like boot laces. I remember how it felt in my hand: cold, smooth, swollen. I brushed sand from its belly. "What's this, Mam?" It rested in the palm of my hand and when she stooped to take it from me, I closed my fist. My treasure, not hers.

"Well I can't tell you what it is if you won't let me see it," she said.

I remember her examining it, holding it toward the sun like an offering. "Well, well," she said, "I do believe you've found a mermaid's purse." I remember the way her long, dark hair tickled my face as she handed it back. Those two words: *mermaid*, *purse*, were enough to set my heart racing.

"You'd think the mermaid would have chosen a different color," I said, disappointed. "Will there be treasure inside?"

My mother laughed, and her face lit up like a real mermaid. "It's called a mermaid's purse, Rowena, but in fact it's an egg-case belonging to a dogfish or a skate."

I remember my profound sense of disappointment. "So no treasure?"

"It's empty," she said. "That was why I held it up to the sun, to check."

I swallowed the words *dogfish* and *egg-case* and focused on *mermaid* and *treasure* instead. After all, Mother might be wrong. "Perhaps the mermaid will come looking for it. I'm going to leave it on the rock for her. She might be watching, and then she might leave me a reward, a jewel or a nugget of gold to say thank you."

"If you wish," my mother said, and I remember the knowing look on her face. The kind of look an adult gives when they're teaching you a lesson. "Or we could take it home, dry it out, and make it into a necklace."

It sounded tempting, but I preferred the thought of a shiny reward. I lay it on a prominent slab of limestone, pinned it down with a bright, white pebble to stop it blowing away, and framed it in a circle of limpet shells. I remember humming the tune to the ballad *The Mermaid* as I worked. I did not know all the words then; just the chorus, though I am able to sing it right through now.

Needless to say, the tide stole back my treasure and brought me no reward, though I checked the rock for days, weeks even.

I do not know why that particular memory sticks in my mind.

I suppose my mother taught me a lesson that day; be grateful for what comes your way and don't expect too much from life. A cynical viewpoint, some might think, especially in one so young.

It is fair to say my mother is both pragmatic and creative. She has one foot planted firmly in the ground, and the other runs with the fairies. An artist in clay is a fitting occupation for such a person since you will not find anything more grounded than clay. And yet she weaves her magic through form and glaze, transforming it into a work of art. Sheer alchemy. I have worked beside her for as long as I can remember. Some of my earliest memories are of us together in the pottery. And she is always singing, though I have noticed her quiet of late. I think it is because she worries about me. Because of me, she is losing her joy.

On the one hand I feel guilty, but at the same time, if she did not force me to attend church this would not have happened. And her, a non-believer. The hypocrisy of it bothers me, though I do see her point about her customers being from the community.

Soon I am to turn twelve and will leave elementary school. She expects me to become her apprentice, but while my heart is with her, my head is not, for I cannot bear it here much longer.

It all started back last Christmas. During his final midnight mass, Father Michael, Reverend of Eglwys y Grog and a very kind man, introduced us to Father Kendrick. Father Michael was retiring and returning to his Cambridgeshire roots. Drunk on the scent of clementine and cloves at the time, I failed to see through Father Kendrick's bright demeanor. I remember him holding aloft the candle and giving us his blessing, his face lit from beneath like the portrait of Jesus which hung on the wall to his right. Considerably younger than Father Michael, Father Kendrick appeared radiant in comparison.

Apart from that, I am able to recall very little about my first impression of Father Kendrick. The swags of holly and ivy which decorated the ends of every pew as well as the altar table were of far greater interest. No mistletoe, though, for the parasitic evergreen bushel is considered Pagan and is therefore banned. What nonsense! Pagan: isn't that the word Mam used to describe Mamgu?

9

IMMORTELLE

The hymns were, of course, sung in Welsh: all Tawel Nos and Gŵyl y Baban. The people of Wales are renowned for their singing and rightly so, and on Christmas Eve our church was filled with song, especially with Mari Howell in attendance. Mari is famous in these parts. They say she has the voice of an angel; she has even sung for King Edward.

But most interesting of all were Mair Richards and Tomos Jones, who sat on the pew in front of me. I found it difficult to concentrate on the words Father Kendrick spoke because my attention was fixed on Mair and Tomos. They were to be married on Christmas morning, the fees more affordable than at other times, and with Tomos being a farmhand, every penny counted. This late in the year meant the church was a frigid cave, yet I swear enough heat radiated from the betrothed couple to warm my complexion. I held out my hands, one to the back of each of their heads, stopping just short of touching. Anticipation, I suppose—the passion of young love, though I should not know of such things at my age.

Their warmth made me sleepy, and as the hands on the clock marched past midnight, my eyelids grew heavy. If it hadn't been for Mam's elbow giving me a poke, and the scent of treacle toffee, I would have fallen asleep. It's tradition here, the toffee. Mamgu Begw from Blaenant Farm makes it every Christmas according to her secret recipe, which includes a guarantee to lose a tooth.

It was not until twelfth night that I first became suspicious of Father Kendrick. A few of the women, my mother among them, had volunteered to take down the church decorations. We risked ill-omen if we left them a day longer, at least according to tradition and our very own bard, William Shakespeare. Candles boxed, Sioned and I were asked to take them to the vestry. Never before had I been inside the vestry as there is sufficient space in the south transept to house the few village children during Sunday school.

A huge oak door, shaped like a pointed arch and with ornate leaded hinges, guarded the entrance. It gave a yawning creak as I pushed it open, adding to the mystery of what lay beyond. The smell of camphor and carbon greeted us—the former stemming from the black cassock which hung on the back of the door, and the latter from an inkwell set upon Father Kendrick's desk. "Smell this," I said, pulling the hem of the garment toward Sioned's face.

She sneezed and wrinkled her nose. "Ych a Fi!" she said. "Reminds me of Mamgu's petticoat drawer." And with that she ran from the room, leaving me all alone.

If only I had followed her. Perhaps none of this would have happened. But I did not, and it did happen.

I peeped around the door, watching as she fled down the aisle toward the women who were busy untying holly wreaths, cursing under their breath in God's house when the holly pricked their frozen fingers. Sioned ran past them and disappeared from sight, no doubt with the aim of locating the toffee tin to see if she might discover a leftover piece. I closed the vestry door, squeezing my eyes tight against its noisy protest.

The tiny room took on a magisterial air once it had me to itself. I began to investigate. There on the desk sat the parish register, open at the page of Mair and Tomos's wedding. With my index finger, I traced Mair's signature—cursive, elegant, and compared to Tomos's cross, a work of art. Would such a thing matter, I wondered. Would her superior intelligence get in the way of their marriage? I vowed then to marry someone at least my equal so that we might discuss subjects greater than the price of wheat and pigs.

Behind the desk stood a bookcase, piled high with bibles and other works of scripture, or so I assumed, for several of the spines were embossed in Latin. I returned to the door and opened it a crack, pressing my ear against it in order to listen. The distant sound of Mam's voice—melodic, jovial, and Sioned's mother Delyth, too. Something must have amused them because they were laughing. In Father Kendrick's absence the church seemed a happier place.

My left hand brushed against his cassock and found something hard. Long and thin—a key perhaps? But I failed to find a pocket. I twisted the cassock until the lining faced me and groped about. Right there, a pocket, concealed within a silken seam. The key slipped into my hand, leaden with guilt. Blood pounded in my ears, my flushed complexion a brazen beacon.

It did not take long to locate the key's companion. A left-hand drawer within the desk, a turn of the key opened it to reveal a large tome embossed in gold letters. I needed both hands to lift it from its hiding place. A sumptuous cover in plum velvet suggested frivolity, and yellowing pages which smelled of ancient dust and almonds (a scent deriving from the chemical benzaldehyde. You see, I do listen to my mother when she teaches me about glazes) urged me to explore its contents. I sped past introductions and index, uncovering works of art, the likes of which I had never seen before.

My mother's art books pale in comparison. Each page, framed in gold leaf and sheathed beneath its own transparent stocking, uncovered a masterpiece. And the images—grotesque, Satanic even, yet oddly alluring for one so curious. One entitled *Hell: The Devil's Muse* depicted a man, naked and muscular, with legs of a satyr and carrying a naked woman on his shoulders toward a figure with a skull in place of a head.

There were others, some even more macabre. I could hardly tear my eyes away. And all the while a question formed in my mind—what on earth was Father Kendrick doing with such a book?

The heat of his body found me first. I noticed the warmth and the smell of stale pipe smoke. I looked up to find Father Kendrick standing over me. Shocked by his sudden appearance, I could not speak. Guilt fixed itself firmly to my face, and my hands fell to my sides. He did not appear to be angered by my intrusion; instead he smirked, though his eyes were black as coals.

"Do you like what you see?" he asked, and I slammed the tome shut. Only then, did he flinch. "Handle it with care. It is valuable," he said, frowning.

I was at a loss for words. How could I possibly explain my actions? "Father, I..." I placed cold hands to my cheeks in an attempt to quell the fire within.

"Hush now," he said, placing a nail-bitten finger to his lips. "I shan't tell if you don't."

And so began the deceit.

CHAPTER THREE

Elinor

I am experimenting with a new glaze when Rowena arrives home from school. Most of my work consists of utilitarian tableware—jugs, bowls, and the odd water set, but my heart lies in studio ceramics. A glance at the clock tells me she is half an hour late and I feel ashamed I did not notice sooner. "Where have you been?" I ask, frowning.

She scowls back at me. "School. Where else?" From her apron pocket she pulls out an apple and takes a bite before propelling herself onto the worktop. "What are you doing?"

I decide to let her tardiness go. Instead of arguing, I smile, pleased she has shown interest. "Trying out a new technique. I want the glaze to crawl over the surface of the pot, similar to lichen on rock. Look, the form is organic, like something you might find at the beach." I hold out the black-slipped vessel for her to see, twisting my wrist so it can be viewed from every angle.

She shrugs, then, "And what's so difficult about it?"

Is she being intentionally obtuse, or does she genuinely not understand? It is difficult to tell since her face gives nothing away. These past few months Rowena has become adept at hiding her feelings. "Well, Rowena, this technique requires a high percentage of magnesium carbonate." I slide the recipe card toward her with the heel of my hand. "I'm not sure the kiln will reach a high enough temperature for it to be successful, so it's a risk."

"And the feldspar creates the crazing," she says.

"You remembered. Well done. We'll make a ceramicist of you yet."

She does not answer; instead, she jumps off the worktop and sidles toward the door.

"Don't you want to see how your first attempt at tin glazing came out from the firing? Quite impressive, I must say." I cheated somewhat in giving her such a task because tin glaze tends not to run and therefore conceals flaws well. But it is important to build on success rather than set her up for a fall. I watch her hesitate before turning back around. The tin-glazed pot is in my hand and I hold it aloft, smiling. A nod of the head, a glance at the vessel, but her eyes do not sparkle as they used to.

"Shall I start tea?" she says, thus ending the conversation.

"You can lay the table. There's a pie in the oven so no need to prepare anything." Then she runs from the pottery, slippery as a glaze.

I have tried my utmost not to make an issue out of Rowena's lack of appetite of late, but I am pleased to see her tuck in to the cheese and onion pie. Another ploy of mine, knowing it is her favorite. I draw the curtains as she scrapes our plates, though there is no need for privacy. Our cottage sits down a narrow lane with no immediate neighbors. Winter solstice has not long passed and the days are short. Before drawing the second curtain, I pause to watch moody clouds race one another. Why are they in such a hurry? The sly old moon winks as they scurry past. She knows there is no reward waiting for them at the end. The kitchen takes on a cozy glow and the scent of soap bubbles replaces the smell of baked onion.

Rowena washes the dishes and I dry. I have raised her to be independent. Elbow deep in suds, she turns to me and says, "Will you tell me about my father?" Her face is flushed. The heat of the water, or embarrassment? My stomach somersaults. This is the question I have been dreading, though I always knew the day would come when she would ask.

"What do you want to know?"

"Anything. Everything." I dry the last cup as she dries her hands.

"Then sit by the fire while I make tea."

She plucks at invisible threads on her pinafore to avoid having to look me in the eye. I will not lie to her, though I may spare her the more sordid details. "You have his nose, though the rest of you belongs to me and Mamgu," I say. It is easier to speak of physicality, but less so of emotional traits. I swallow the words *and his cunning and willfulness*. In her, such traits are tolerable, even amusing at times. In him, they were not so.

"Your father was powerful and wealthy, Rowena. He co-owned the pottery in Staffordshire that employed me." Still she does not look at me. Instead she follows the dance of the flames. "At the age of fourteen I began work as a painter there, but was fortunate enough to attend evening classes at the same time because Mamgu invested every penny she could spare in my education. Soon the quality of work I produced impressed the management and it wasn't long before I was given the opportunity to work with gilding—a job tenaciously guarded by the men."

She breathes a shuddering sigh and her shoulders relax. I find myself wondering if this is what has upset her of late. Perhaps she has been harboring thoughts about her roots and felt unable to ask. "One day I came to the attention of your father when a rude remark was made about me by one of the men. From then on, your father favored me, and I must confess I found his attention flattering. I was young, you see. Young and foolish."

"You were just fourteen."

"No. By the time I met your father, I had worked at the factory for almost three years, so I was seventeen." I flush, knowing he was fifteen years my senior, but I shall omit this detail. We sit in silence for a few minutes, and I wonder how best to proceed. "Our story is simple, Rowena, and unfortunately an all too common one."

"Did you marry him?"

My breath catches at her abruptness, and I find myself embarrassed by what I have to say next. "He was already married, though he kept the fact secret for a long time. Until it was too late. Until I had already fallen in love with him and was pregnant with you."

Her response shocks me to the core and steals my breath. "Then it is true what they say. I am a bastard." She hugs herself around the middle. For comfort, or to keep me distant?

"Who called you such a thing, Rowena?" The coal spits, and a spark burns my hand in reprimand, causing me to cry out in pain. But she does not flinch.

"It does not matter who said it. The truth is all that matters."

I am hurt; her words are a physical pain like a knife to the guts. "Well, whoever said such a thing is evil and ignorant. No child has ever been more loved or wanted as you are." But I know the conversation is not over. There is worse to come.

"How did we end up here?"

I spit on my finger and rub the red mark on my hand, though the pain has dissipated. "When I broke the news to him, he panicked. Terrified that his wife would find out about our relationship and leave him, he reacted selfishly." I smooth down my skirts, embarrassed and saddened by what I have to say. I reach across to take Rowena's hand, but she pulls away: angry, wilful. "You must not underestimate how difficult it was for me, Rowena. The most difficult time of my life. Then Mamgu fell ill, adding to the strain. She was sick, very sick, Rowena. It all got too much for me and I—"

I stop mid-sentence because Rowena is crying. Tears the size of raindrops tumble down her face and spill onto her pinafore, unhindered. And yet she is silent. I kneel before her, and retrieve a handkerchief from my pocket. She allows me to touch her. "This is why I haven't told you before," I say. "I didn't want to hurt you."

"Did he ever see me?" She looks at me for the first time, searching for the truth in my eyes. I cannot bring myself to lie.

"No. I never saw him again. He sent the factory manager to Mamgu's house with a letter stating my employment was terminated."

"Terminated?"

"Ended. As well as the letter, the envelope contained a check made out in my name, enough for us to start over again. And when Mamgu died not long after you were born, that's what we did. We came here, back to the place of Mamgu's birth."

"Did he try to find us?"

She wants to think he did. I understand this, but it is not the case. "No, Rowena. He never tried to contact us."

"But did you tell him where we were going? Perhaps he changed his mind. He might want to see me." She sits on the edge of the seat, all arms and chin, about to spring at me.

"Rowena," I say in a firm voice. As much as I don't want her hurt, I will not allow her to be disillusioned. "I left a forwarding address with my solicitor. As I said, your father was powerful. If he wanted to make contact, he would have done so."

She says nothing for a few moments and dabs at her eyes with a handkerchief before delivering the blow. "By the way, I've been thinking. When I leave school this summer, I want to go into service far away from here. I don't want to work in the pottery."

Wide awake. The Atlantic winds have chased away the clouds and the moon is smiling. She is at peace. Lucky moon. There is so much more I did not tell Rowena. It seems her mind is poisoned against me enough without having to administer the final drop. Perhaps one day, when she is older and has experienced a different kind of love, she will understand. I will tell her then about her half-brother, a year older than she is. I will explain why I have a scar above my left eyebrow. I may even show her the contract her father forced me to sign, which prevents either of us from staking claim to a penny of his wealth. As far as he was concerned, the check he provided exempted him of all future responsibility.

CHAPTER FOUR

Rowena

The apples that grow in the front garden of The Rectory are the sweetest I have ever tasted. Laden with daubs of shiny red, the tree is an irresistible temptress straight out the book of Genesis. Father Michael never minded us children picking them as we passed on our way home from school. In fact he encouraged it, saying God's good grace should never go to waste. But what about Father Kendrick? Would the apple once again become the forbidden fruit? With a furtive glance toward the house, I reached up and pulled.

"The apple never falls far from the tree." I turned to see Father Kendrick standing on the porch. Right hand ripe with evidence, I knew in an instant this was not the first time he had caught me stealing, if taking a key from a secret pocket could be considered such.

"I'm sorry, Father," I said, red skinned as the fruit. "Father Michael let us take them. I thought perhaps—"

He strode toward me with a blank expression. "Did he indeed? Then I suppose I shall have to do the same."

"Thank you, Father," I said. "I'd best be getting home." Before he could say more, I dashed away, but his words stuck in my throat, *the apple never falls far from the tree.* It wasn't a fallen apple I had chosen but a large specimen still attached to the bough.

The following day I remembered to ask Miss Price, my teacher, what it meant. Her explanation perturbed me somewhat. It suggested condemnation of my mother. I decided not to mention it to her, just in case.

A week or so passed by before I saw him again. A week of incessant autumn rain, the kind of weather one does not dawdle in. As usual, Sioned and I parted ways at the end of Quarry Row, and I began the walk toward our cottage alone. The Rectory stood at the bottom of the lane, guarding the entrance, making it impossible to avoid.

The afternoon had seen the end of the downpour and the sky blushed pink, embarrassed by her outburst. As I turned the corner, a rainbow arched in the distance, cutting the field in two. Marshmallow clouds kissed the brow of the hill and a sense of contentment caught me off-guard.

"Here, take these." In one hand, Father Kendrick held a basket and in the other, a book. "Your mother can make a pie," he said, holding the basket out to me. It was filled to the brim with apples.

"Thank you, Father," I said.

"And I thought you might be interested in reading this," he said, holding out the book, "though perhaps it might be best if you keep it to yourself for now." When I hesitated, he frowned. "I assume you are able to read?"

"Of course," I said rather indignantly. My reading scores are the highest in the class and I am proud to share the fact. "I read both Welsh and English very well."

"Glad to hear it," he said, handing me the book. The volume was slim, just right for hiding in the folds of my pinafore. "Written by a member of the clergy," he said, grinning. "Though the story is about a man who sells his soul to the devil."

In one hand I held a basket of red apples; in the other, Volume One of *Melmoth the Wanderer.* From what Father Kendrick had said about it, I could not decide which tempted me more.

IMMORTELLE

That night, my belly full of apple pie, I made room to devour a portion of the book loaned to me by the reverend.

I read slowly at first, the story being more complex than I was used to, but paragraph by paragraph, page by page, I began to unfold a tale about a man named John Melmoth, reported to have been seen on several occasions after his death. It suggested the supernatural and hooked me in like a carp.

Further chapters led me to discover that an Englishman named Stanton wrote of his sightings of Melmoth the Wanderer, which angered Melmoth. As a result, Melmoth prophesied Stanton would end up in the lunatic asylum known as Bedlam, even though he would be sane. The prophecy, of course, came true. Melmoth visited Stanton at the asylum and promised him his freedom on condition he sell his soul to the devil.

Never before had I read of such things. Lost in the story, my heart leapt when my mother entered my room to say goodnight, though I was shrewd enough to have disguised it behind a copy of *Jane Eyre.* "Not too long now, Rowena," she said. "You have school in the morning." As if I didn't know. She can be an insufferable know-all at times.

I read until my eyes burned with fatigue, unable to put the book down. A ghost which left proof of his visit in the form of a bruise to the wrist. A shipwreck off the Irish coast. A death from a cliff fall: accident or murder? I could not wait for the following night to come, in order to continue reading.

Just one thing bothered me, a similar question to the one which nagged when I found the book of demonic art in Father Kendrick's desk. Why did a man of the cloth see fit to provide a young girl with such ghastly reading material?

Melmoth the Wanderer became the catalyst for my journey into the unknown. I suppose I am to blame for my own downfall since I put my faith in the reverend. But now I am afraid. Afraid that things have gone too far, taken too sinister a turn, and I do not know how to retreat. I fear that if I do not get away soon, I will fall victim to his spell once and for all.

To the outside world Father Kendrick presents as a man of God, a man in whom they put their trust, but I have seen another side, and yet I am unable to tear myself away. Hook, line, and sinker, I flounder in his keepnet. If I am able to stay strong for a few months longer, until I finish school, I might be able to leave this place and go into service somewhere far away.

It is difficult to put into words the hold he has over me, for it is not physical. Not once has he ever touched me inappropriately or even suggested such a thing, and yet I feel tainted. The compulsion to visit him is an emotional one. There is a power to the man I cannot put my finger on.

Most days I rush home from school so I can spend a few minutes in his company. No longer do I dawdle with Sioned gossiping about the other children. And even when I am late, my mother hardly notices, so immersed in her own art is she. So the deceit has been easy.

The Rectory, to me, is a grown-up version of the witch's cottage in the story of "Hansel and Gretel." In place of gingerbread and confection there are paintings and pentagrams, skulls and candle sconces, all of which are hidden in a room that he tells me was once a priest-hide. A wall panel to the left of the fireplace in the drawing room leads to the cellar. A secret room of sorts.

I have witnessed firsthand Father Kendrick's alchemy. An illustrated grimoire lists his experiments, which even to my mind grow increasingly labyrinthine. He tells me they allow him to gain greater magical powers, and with my own eyes I have witnessed him cause a blooming Alexandra to wither and die with a single drop from a pipette.

On one occasion I saw a gull's wing healed by the application of a salve, one which smelled of comfrey and bitter herbs, and to which three drops of the gull's own blood was added. The salve was then applied not to the bird's wing but to the blade of the knife that caused the injury. I swear on my mother's life, not a week later we set the bird free on the wing.

I suppose he has demonstrated a certain kindness toward me these past months, and yet I rarely laugh in his company. I wonder why it is me he has chosen but do not wish to dwell on the reason in case his motives are ulterior. Perhaps he considers me rebellious, like him, for his actions defy the teachings of the church. Perhaps he sees me as a kindred spirit.

Or perhaps he is taking advantage of my vulnerability. I have no father to defend me, and yet there are others in the same position and he has not approached them, at least not as far as I am aware. He spoke to me of my father, asked whether I had any dealings with him, and really I was able to tell him next to nothing. This is why I chose to talk to my mother about him. "If I am right, and you were conceived out of wedlock," Father Kendrick said, "then some would call you a bastard, though it is an unkind word to use." Although he smiled, I felt tainted by his words, inferior, and when my mother confirmed his suspicion, I took my anger out on her, though I do not know why. Perhaps it is because I cannot be angry with my father since I have no clue as to who or where he is.

Two things concern me of late. The first is my growing obsession with the books, artworks, and alchemy Father Kendrick shares with me, for they have opened up a world I didn't know existed. A world of sin, power, and desire. I find it difficult to pay attention to everyday things such as schoolwork and chores. Even the chemical magic my mother weaves in the pottery is not as enticing as this. I am unable to eat or sleep, and I am torn between confiding in my mother or keeping my secrets close.

But there is something else which concerns me, something I discovered just recently.

On occasion, when Father Kendrick's attention is elsewhere, I am able to get a closer look at the various artefacts and curiosities he has on shelves within the secret room. I do not touch, of course, though I would if he were not near. I handle only what he passes to me. He makes no bones of the fact that many things are unique and irreplaceable.

A week or so ago, a new specimen jar on one of the shelves caught my eye. It stood beside a book entitled, *The Potency of Corpse Medicine*, a title I longed to browse, though dared not ask to borrow. Wadding half-filled the jar and sitting on top of the wadding were two small, semi-transparent objects, each about the size of a micro mollusc. Father Kendrick must have noticed my scrutiny of the jar as he called me back to the table on the pretence of showing me his latest collection of feathers.

A few days later, Mam and I visited Katrin Morgan to see her newborn baby, and as I held the baby's hand, I realized what the objects in the jar were: the tiny nails of a newborn. If I am correct, and it is not just the fancy of a young girl, then Father Kendrick has gone too far. But how might he have acquired such a thing? And what does he intend to do with them? I cannot eradicate the image from my mind, nor the fact that the jar sat alongside a book on corpse medicine. Though it is not a term I am familiar with, it suggests something terrible.

My imagination is fuelled by the whispered conversation I overheard between my mother and Katrin. They spoke of a woman from the village whose baby died soon after birth a few weeks ago. They said how the mother, whose name I did not recognize, was inconsolable and how the baby's father thought it best if the baby's body remained at church until the funeral, rather than at home.

I lie awake at night, picturing the reverend with pliers in his hand, removing the nails from a dead baby with a callous grin on his face. In my dreams, the baby is alive; it screams at the top of its lungs as blood trickles down its tiny fingers. I wake up sweating, determined to discover the truth, but in the morning my fear returns.

Over and over again, I picture the things I have seen and heard whilst in his company. Often he has spoken of the power of the innocent and it makes me wonder: is it possible for anything to be more innocent than a newborn child? The thought of him acquiring such a thing by anything other than proper means causes me such distress, and yet what proper means could there be? Of course it would be possible for Father Kendrick to have removed the nails of the newborn whilst it lay in repose at Eglwys y Grog, but why would he do such an evil thing? Unless, of course, he has begun to experiment with corpse medicine.

What if I am implicated in all this? What if through my involvement with him I am seen to be of similar mind? My mother would never forgive me, nor would I forgive myself. And that is why I cannot wait for these next months to pass. Then I will have an excuse to move away—away from temptation—for as much as I find such things abhorrent, I am still compelled to visit The Rectory on a frequent basis.

I have thought about the things in the jar time and again, and have reached my decision: I intend to be brave. The next time I see him, I shall inquire as to what they are and try to glean his reaction. If he admits they are what I believe them to be, then I shall confide in my mother. I shall lay my cards on the table and leave the rest to her.

If on the other hand he lies, or indeed has a plausible explanation as to what they might be, then I shall take it from there.

IMMORTELLE

One thing I am certain of—I cannot go on like this much longer.

PART TWO

CHAPTER FIVE

Elinor

The darkness shifts and merges until it becomes human-shaped. An indistinct black mass with a nodding head looms over me. A voice, amplified yet muffled, like the wearing-off of anaesthetic, demands my attention. Where am I? My head spins and I desperately try to find logic within my surroundings. I am on the floor of the pottery. Something warm and wet trickles down the left side of my face. I touch it and the palm of my hand comes away bloody.

And then I remember.

"Water, Father," a voice says. "She needs water."

I try to scream, but my tongue and lips refuse to obey. I utter a moan. Let me sleep. I do not want to surface. Not now that I have remembered.

"All right, Elinor. You're all right."

The man in black puts an arm around my shoulders and helps me to sit. His tall hat has slipped to one side. Under different circumstances, I might find it amusing. Blood trickles into my mouth, salty, warm, and I spit. My hand goes again to my head and I feel the lump. I do not care. "No," I moan, "You lie!"

Another black figure arrives, carrying a glass of water. He crouches close and I recognize him. It is Father Kendrick. Of course it would be. It was he who knocked the door to the pottery, accompanied by the policeman.

"Drink, Elinor."

I push his hand away and try to stand, but my legs refuse to do as I command.

And then I scream. I hear it, as though it comes from someone else, somewhere else. Guttural, gurgling, like a wild animal.

The faces of the men sharpen. The policeman is drawn and pale, like a ghost. His expression is one of concern. Father Kendrick's face is flushed. His dark eyes refuse to focus on my face for longer than is necessary and his mouth is dry. I know this because he repeatedly tries to wet his lips with his tongue.

I am dreaming. I hope I am dreaming. Wake up! My hands and feet flail at the ground, desperate to help me stand, and this time I manage it. Gravity causes blood to pour down my face, blinding me, and for a brief second I imagine how I must look. Like a madwoman, no doubt.

"Sit down, Elinor," the policeman says in an assertive voice. He drags a stool toward me with his free hand, the sound of metal scraping along the floor sets my teeth on edge. His voice is firm but kind, and I do as he says. He turns to Father Kendrick. "Go fetch the doctor." And Father Kendrick makes a swift exit, as if he were waiting for an excuse to leave.

The policeman grabs a cloth to stem the flow of blood from my head, but the one on the worktop is clay-choked. He holds my hand. He is lost for words, so instead he shushes my moans like a caring parent.

I panic. The urge to run to Rowena overwhelms me and I dash for the door. The strength of a lion—wild and untamed. I must go to her. She needs me! Every second I waste here is lost.

"Rowena!" Two steps and I am pulled back.

"You can go to her as soon as the doctor has seen to you," the policeman says. "That gash on your head is nasty. It needs looking at."

"Where is she?" I spit the bloody words, pulling my arm from his grasp.

"Please, Elinor. I understand how you must be feeling, but there is nothing you can do."

"I must go to her. She needs me!" Tiny droplets of blood fly from my mouth as I speak. They land on his cheek, in stark contrast to his pallor, but he makes no attempt to wipe them away. He sighs, the weight of the world on his bony shoulders.

"There is nothing you can do for her," he says. "She is peaceful. We made sure of it."

I have a vague memory of them telling me she is in the church. I close my eyes and picture her lying on the altar table, draped in white. But that is far from reality. The panic is overwhelming and just as I make a second attempt to escape, the door opens and Doctor Richards enters, closely followed by Father Kendrick.

"My dear girl," he says, and I collapse against his chest.

"They say she's dead, Doctor. It's not true, is it?" More than anything I want him to deny the fact. I want him to declare both the policeman and the priest liars and curse them to hell. But he does not. Instead, he glances down at his feet, then at me. And his eyes speak for him.

"She is at peace, Elinor." He takes my hand in his. "I have seen her. Now let me see to that cut, then we can talk."

I turn my head and vomit into the clay bucket.

An incessant drizzle falls as we make our way down the lane and onto the track which leads to the church. My skin is baptized by its gentle cooling. No one speaks, not even the birds. Instead they bow their heads in sympathy. Leaden legs fall forward, one step at a time, like an automaton. My innards are a pit of waste and I expect to wake up at any moment.

As we draw near, the gray sea rolls in to greet us and black-faced sheep bleat a solemn song. As we pass through the gate, I see the gravestones as if for the first time. Stone slabs with meaningless words inscribed on their faces are the only memorial to those once most loved. I try to console myself with the thought that there cannot be a more peaceful place in all the world to spend eternity, for the view of the cliffs and the sea is sublime. But my thoughts turn darker, surely Rowena will not soon lie amongst them? I cannot bring myself to believe it. The image threatens to choke me. Panic rises, and I can hardly breathe.

IMMORTELLE

As the four of us arrive on the threshold, Father Kendrick fumbles for his keys. The door to the church is locked. Father Kendrick never locks the door. It dawns on me that he did so because within the benign-looking building lies the body of my daughter, and he did not want to risk anyone else stumbling upon her until she has been taken care of. I tremble from head to toe and cannot swallow or speak. I think perhaps I might faint again, but the policeman, Constable Matthews, holds me firm by the elbow and tells me to breathe slowly. "Are you sure you want to do this, Elinor? Why don't you wait until—"

"I'm certain." I am not, though. In fact, I have never been so terrified in my whole life. The whole thing is surreal.

The click of the key in the lock sounds like a gunshot. Father Kendrick leads the way, locking the door behind us. The smell of wood polish and ancient stone, and there's something else—incense. Doctor Richards makes a last-ditch attempt to change my mind. "Really, Elinor. I think you'd be better off waiting until the coroner has—"

"No. Take me to her."

"I must warn you, it's not a pretty sight. The water... it—"

"Water?" This is the first time anyone has mentioned water.

Doctor Richards takes a deep breath and his nostrils flare. He exchanges glances with Constable Matthews. "They discovered her body face down in the trough, though she may not have drowned. We must not jump to conclusions, not until the coroner has—"

I barge past him, desperate to see my daughter.

CHAPTER SIX

It is late February and the banks bordering the hedgerows are sugar-frosted with snowdrops, Rowena's favorite flower. I pause at the gate on my way to the pottery and close my eyes, listening for her voice. "Look how delicate they are, Mam. It means spring's not far round the corner, doesn't it?" So crisp, so clear, I am compelled to turn and look for her.

But she is not here, not in the garden. Instead she lies in a coffin within the cottage, dressed in a shroud of white and scattered with calendula and mimosa, known for their sweet fragrance. These past two days have been spent by her side. I have talked to her, begged her to come back, but she lies as still and serene as a statue and refuses to do as I ask. If I stay in the room much longer, I will lose my mind, and so I have decided to spend a few hours in the pottery making an immortelle for her grave.

There are a few who will condemn me for choosing snowdrops, for it is said they are a sign of ill omen—a warning of death. Well, that has already occurred. There is no worse to come.

IMMORTELLE

I cannot say how I stop my hands from trembling as I mold the clay, but somehow I manage it.

Each snowdrop consists of three pure-white petals. The stems I will shape from sturdy wire before attaching them to ceramic ovaries, glazed green: three parts copper oxide to one part chromium oxide. In place of a stigma, I will attach a tiny bell. If she wishes, she will be able to call me from the grave. I will listen for her ring both night and day.

I shape a base from clay bedded with sprigs of swan's-neck thyme-moss, so true to life I expect it to spring back to my touch. But it does not, for the moss is made of clay and cannot therefore respond to touch.

The light is fading, daylight hours short, and I have spent enough time away from my beloved girl for now.

Within two days, Rowena's immortelle is almost complete, except for one thing—a young starling. Her immortelle must include a starling, for starlings are known to carry messages from the spirit world. When she is ready to talk to me, it will ferry her voice. Already moulded and bisque-fired, the bird is ready to glaze. Adding the detail will test my patience, but I am determined it must look perfect.

Glazes mixed, my workbench is prepared with an assortment of fine brushes, clean sponge, and the turntable on which the bird rests. It cannot yet sing, but in time it might. And then, just as I am about to apply the base color, I picture Rowena lying in her coffin in our sitting room and I am overwhelmed with the desire to be with her again.

Why am I wasting time in the pottery when in two days' time she will be taken from me and I will never see her again? The day after tomorrow she is to be buried and will be lost to me forever. I take a few deep breaths and fight the urge to run back indoors. My stomach is a knotted root, strands of fibrous muscle balled tight. Sweat beads on my upper lip and my limbs turn to jelly.

Eventually the feeling passes, and I calm down. If I am guilty of neglect, it is because I failed to worry when she was half an hour late from school, and not because I am in here preparing her immortelle while she lies dead.

A moan escapes my throat, and my hands grasp the edge of the worktop so hard my knuckles glow white. But I must complete this task. It feels urgent, like a speck of compensation for my overwhelming sense of guilt. I pour a glass of cold water and feel it trickle its way toward the tight knot at my centre. I am empty. I have not eaten enough to keep this starling alive, but I deserve to suffer.

I sit in front of the unglazed starling, stare into sightless eyes, and go back over the coroner's words. Inconclusive. A verdict of accidental death, and in proclaiming such a thing he spared me the worst, for I could have been implicated further in her death. What shocked me most was discovering that the contents of her stomach included apple and traces of arsenic. Arsenic! Not enough to prove fatal they believe, nor did she drown, not strictly speaking. The water was a contributing factor, or so they say. The coroner believes the poison brought on sickness, which encouraged her to drink from the animal trough, though I do not accept the fact. So many questions remain unanswered. Why was she in the field? Did she mess with the glaze chemicals? In my heart I know she did not, but my head reminds me how unhappy she seemed of late, how anxious.

I am certain some in the village blame me. They know the pottery contains the ingredient that contributed to her death, and I have neither the strength nor will to convince them otherwise. Why should I implore them to believe me when I say such chemicals are kept under lock and key? Do I care that they think me remiss for teaching her the glazing process? No, they can think what they will. I do not care. I refuse to believe Rowena knowingly inflicted harm on herself, for if it is true, then how did she come to be found face down in a water trough fit for the cows?

Misadventure—not murder. The post-mortem found insufficient evidence of any sign of struggle. Once they released her body, I carried out my own examination, though it tortured me to do so. I checked every inch of flesh, washed her and dressed her in a shroud with my own hands, and like them found little in the way of bruising. Gwyneth from the farm helped me to lay her out, her old hands as kind and gentle as Mamgu's. She offered to do it alone, but I refused because I needed to see for myself.

I force the memory from my mind, swallow the bile that burns my throat, and focus on the task in hand...

What color is a starling? I know I should glaze it brown since it is winter and at this time of year, it would be wearing its winter plumage, but I cannot bring myself to do so. Rowena loved color. When she was a little girl, she saw color in everything—the muted grays and pinks of scallops, the lapis blue of the mussel, the cinnamon tinged petals of bird's foot. I remember her disappointment when she found a mermaid's purse because it was black.

So I shall glaze the starling for summer: iridescent feathers of purple and green, brilliant white spots on its breast, and a bright yellow beak with a pale pink base. Once glazed, I shall add tiny seed pearls to its chest which will catch the light through the glass dome of the immortelle.

Among my supplies are glass-beaded eyes. Acquired from a taxidermist friend, I hid them away like a magpie, knowing that one day they would find their purpose. I never imagined it to be this.

Rowena's immortelle will be a work of art, but no less than she deserves. It is all I have to offer.

My work for the day is done, and now I will return to the cottage and spend the evening at her side.

Several hours have passed since I saw her last, but nothing has changed. Her beautiful face bears the same expression as it did when I left—one of restful peace.

Each time I enter the sitting room I imagine she will sit up, rub her eyes and smile, and it will all be a mistake.

But she does not.

I have a snippet of news to share with her before I retire to bed. Gwyneth called at the pottery earlier to say that Mari Howell is home from London and is to sing at Rowena's funeral. I hope she will hear Mari's voice, for I know how much she admired it.

It is the evenings I find hardest. Regardless of their private thoughts, most people from the village have been kind. Throughout the day I have been inundated with unannounced visitors and gestures of goodwill. The larder is laden with tins of cake and home-baked biscuits which I cannot stomach. If it weren't for visitors, they would go to waste. Rowena would have had rich pickings; all her favorites are here. I would give my life for her to be able to taste them.

I glance at the clock on the mantle, then remember Gwyneth winding it back to match the time of death, as is customary, which was estimated to be around four o'clock. In two days' time the clock can be rewound and life will resume without Rowena. At least it will for others. For me, it will never be the same.

I have not seen myself in days, for the mirrors are draped in crepe to prevent Rowena's spirit getting trapped inside the looking glass. Would she have believed in such traditions? I think perhaps she would since she had a propensity toward the macabre. I wonder if she recalls our conversation about ghosts? I remember her telling me how Mamgu's ghost came to her and said everything would be all right. Did she lie, Rowena? Or did you?

Now I must kiss my sweet girl goodnight, for I have Mamgu's notes to study. If I am to attempt the ritual I have planned for tomorrow, I must be prepared. With the immortelle complete and Mamgu's instructions, I hope to capture her spirit once and for all before it takes flight.

CHAPTER SEVEN

This morning my nerves are in tatters. Sleep evaded me for most of the night, and when eventually it came, I dreamed of Rowena as a young girl. The summer's day shone bright, and as we made our way to the beach she pointed toward the church. "Look, Mam," she said, shielding her eyes from the sun. "A white church."

"Don't you recognize it, Rowena?" I said. "It's our church. We go there every Sunday."

She frowned and shook her head. "Don't be silly. It's not the same one. I want to go see it."

I thought perhaps she did not recognize it from this angle, so to humour her, we changed direction and headed toward it. Her hand was warm in mine, small and frail, and I felt a surge of love so strong it made me moan.

"What's wrong, Mam?" she said, turning toward me, and as she did so, something changed. Skin veined blue, eyes fixed and teary, she began to choke. I grabbed hold of her and thumped the heels of my hands against her lungs. A plume of dark water spewed from her throat, frothed at my feet, and the noise! Gurgling and choking, she gasped for air. My grip on her loosened, the skin slick, and I could not hold on to her. I woke then, in a bath of sweat and my face streaked with tears.

Just a dream, I try to console myself. But it is not. The nightmare is real.

Every single day, before I open my eyes, the shock of her death hits like a wave, and again and again I am swept away with the tide.

Tonight, once her immortelle is complete, I shall attempt a feat of alchemy which, to the best of my knowledge, has never before been performed. But first I must find a way to get through another day of well-wishers, one of whom is Father Kendrick, for it is he who will conduct tomorrow's funeral ceremony. I have not seen him since the day Rowena died. He has kept well away, corresponding on funeral arrangements via notes ferried by Gwyneth. I dread seeing him, but at the same time there are questions I wish him to answer. Quite how I will find the strength to ask them, I do not know.

The bitter tang of herbal tea awakens my palate, and for the first time in days I manage to eat, though it is meager. Frost blankets the ground, and as I crunch my way toward the pottery, Rowena's robin is perched on the gatepost waiting for me. I have neglected him. Rowena would be disappointed, so I return to the cottage for some stale cake and crumble it in front of the porch. "Watch over her while I work," I whisper, and he tilts his head to the side before pecking at the offering. He will do as I ask.

The door to the kiln opens with a groan, reluctant to wake from its warm, gem-filled bed. The starling is magnificent. As I lift it out, iridescent feathers shimmer purple to green and its beak is tinged with a healthy blush. I am eager to add the final touches: glass eyes for the gift of sight, and tiny seed pearls, like those on a Fabergé egg, will add an air of majesty, for she is my princess.

Now all that remains is to arrange the elements in the form of a miniature garden, for that is what I hope Rowena's immortelle will be.

I am deep in thought when Father Kendrick knocks on the door to the pottery. I had forgotten about his visit, though in any case I have no clue what the time is. Still, I do not wish him to think me rude or ungrateful and should at least have prepared tea. Discomfort oozes from him. His expression is bleak, and I wonder whose pallor appears closer to the grave—his or my own. "Come in, Father." I hold the door ajar but do not offer my hand which is covered in green paint.

He steps over the threshold, head bowed low, and scans the workroom. The last time he came, he brought the most dreadful news. He must be thinking the same. His gaze falls on the immortelle. "What do we have here?" he asks, with a weak attempt at a smile. In all likelihood, he is pleased to find me able to focus my attention on something creative.

"It is to be Rowena's immortelle."

His face falls, and he frowns. "Immortelle? I believe she will be the first to have such a frivolous memorial at Eglwys y Grog." He flushes and tries to bite back the words, but it is too late.

"You do not approve, Father?" What is it about the man that causes my hackles to rise? It is a good thing I do not believe in God, or He would strike me down.

"Not at all, Elinor. You mistake me." He steps closer, examining the immortelle in detail. "It's just that folk around here tend to choose more simple memorials—something more sedate, shall we say? More traditional." He wipes his hands on the front of his cassock as though cleansing himself of any connection with the immortelle. "But you must do as you wish."

Anger twists my lip. "The snowdrops, Father, they symbolize Rowena's purity." I am certain he flinches at my words.

"And the bird?"

"A starling, Father. They make good messengers." I resist the temptation to tell him they are great mimics, capable of taking on the voice of those they are accustomed to, though I believe he gets the gist of my meaning because his frown lines deepen further.

"I've come to check you are prepared for tomorrow?" he asks, swallowing his obvious distaste. "No doubt the service will be very difficult for you, though you must remember Rowena is in God's care now, and a funeral is our way of giving thanks for her life."

My stomach churns and I take a deep breath. "Actually, Father, there are a few questions I would like to ask. Will you come inside for a cup of tea?"

Rowena's robin eyes him with suspicion from the holly tree. The bird turns his back on the reverend, and fluffs his tail, which makes me smile. The berries are all but gone, though the tree's prickly foliage is as robust as ever. "I suppose you know the berries of a holly tree are toxic to humans?" I say, causing him to wince again. Why do I feel the need to provoke him? What good will come of it? I think it is because I am bitter. If he had found Rowena earlier, things might have turned out differently and she may still be with me. If I am honest, I am also angry because he is able to put his faith in an omnipotent being and I cannot. Any scrap of faith I had has been swept away by Rowena's death.

A wreath of laurel and yew is tied to the door with white ribbons: a sign there has been a death in the family. As he draws close, a gust of wind whips at the strands, sending them into an agitated dance. Even the wreath mistrusts him. The bright, spicy scent of laurel wafts toward us. "Did you know the scent of laurel is meant to help when one feels sad or distressed, Father?" Such beliefs are Pagan in origin and I am aware it will provoke him further.

He shakes his head. "I did not, but I do know the Ancient Greeks believed laurel had the ability to cleanse the spirit." He clears his throat. "But Rowena's spirit is not in need of cleansing, I'm sure."

As we enter the hallway, the unmistakable odor of death greets us, despite her coffin being draped in mimosa and calendula. My stomach churns, for I still cannot believe it has happened.

Neither of us speak as we enter the sitting room. The tainted air is tangible. It seems to take on a visible quality as he approaches the coffin. He looks down on her, but I cannot see his expression. "Such a tragedy," he says, and his breath shudders. "I'm so sorry, Elinor. I hope that once tomorrow is over, you can begin to pick up the pieces of your life." His words are spoken in earnest, yet I find myself wanting to scoff, so I shove my hands deep into my pockets and pinch myself as a warning to toe the line.

"Come, Father," I say. "We shall take tea in the kitchen." He makes the sign of the cross on Rowena's forehead, mumbles words of prayer, and we leave the room. I close the door behind him, for I do not wish her to hear the things I have to say.

The tea is poured in Mamgu's best china. He glances toward the dresser, which I have prepared in readiness for tomorrow's guests. I follow his gaze. Of course, the whiskey. He is known to enjoy a tipple. "Would you like a tot of whiskey in your tea, Father?" I hope he consents; perhaps it will loosen his tongue.

"If you insist," he says, his dark eyes brightening, and I comply with a goodly measure. "Now then, is there anything you need to ask about tomorrow's proceedings?"

My stomach churns and I fight back the tears. I have not cried yet—not really. I am afraid once the tears start to flow, they will never stop. I gulp my tea. It is too hot and burns my throat, which is no less than I deserve. "It's not tomorrow I worry about, Father. I mean, I'm dreading it, but what concerns me most is my inability to relinquish the sense of guilt."

"You must not blame yourself, Elinor. Life can be cruel, and guilt is part of the grieving process. You are not to blame." He reaches out to take my hand, but I pull away.

I reach for the whiskey bottle. "A little more, Father?" To my surprise, he takes the bottle from me and helps himself. *So it's not just Irish priests who enjoy a drink, then.* I take a deep breath and prepare to ask the question which has been burning inside me all week. "What I wanted to ask, Father, was whether or not you think Rowena might have been saved if—" I cannot finish the sentence. The words stick in my throat.

"Well?"

"If she had been found sooner. I mean, I cannot understand what she was doing in the field at that time of day." My tea has cooled somewhat, and I gulp it down. "I've gone over and over the coroner's words, but none of it makes sense. If only the farmhand had found her sooner, or you—"

He shakes his head, and raises a hand to stop me. "You must not torture yourself like this, Elinor. Nothing can change what has happened."

"But the water, Father. So cold! And from an animal trough. She would not have drunk from it unless desperate, or not of sound mind."

His glass is drained, and I sense his eagerness to leave. The ranting of a bereaved mother causes him discomfort, but I feel no sympathy. As a minister, it is his place to deal with such emotions. "Listen, Elinor. These are questions only God can answer. Would Rowena want you to distress yourself in this way?"

"But I need to know, Father." I am almost shouting. "Trust me, I will never give up until I know what happened to her. Not as long as I have breath in my body."

He stands, and slides the chair under the table. "I must go now. I have another visit to make, but I will see you at eleven in the morning. In the meantime, if there is anything you need—"

I grip his wrist, and he flinches at my touch. "There is one thing I must know, Father. When you pulled her from the water… her expression—did she seem?" I am afraid of the answer. Afraid of not knowing the answer. He waits for me to find my courage. "Did she appear frightened?" A tear rolls down my cheek, and I let it travel.

His shoulders sag and I know he finds it difficult to look at me. "Elinor, you mustn't torture yourself this way."

"But I need to know!" My voice is raised, frantic almost. "Please!"

He drags out the chair and sits back down. "You want me to be honest?" I nod, and our eyes lock. He takes a deep breath before answering. "I did not consider Rowena's expression at the time. There were more important things to focus on. Looking back, I think I was in shock, the same goes for Rhys, the farmhand who found her. As you know, I happened to be leaving the church when I noticed him waving and calling. The wind whipped his words out to sea, but I could sense his urgency." He takes my hand and this time, I let him. "You must know that I ran to him as fast as I could." His eyes plead with me to believe him. "As I drew close, I realized he was struggling to hold her above the water. He tried his best, but she was a—" He glances down, realizing he has not chosen the best phrase.

I finish the sentence for him. "A dead weight."

He nods. "I lifted her legs and together we lay her on the ground." His eyes flash dark, and I can see it is not easy for him. "We tried, Elinor. We tried to get the water from her lungs, but little came up. We were too late. She was beyond help."

My face is a river. Silent tears gush unhindered. He offers me a handkerchief, and I take it. "So you cannot say—"

"Perhaps we did wrong. Perhaps we should have left her on

the grass until the constable and the doctor had been sent for, but it seemed cruel. The bitter wind, the roar of the ocean below. She seemed exposed." He shudders a little at the memory. "We thought it best to carry her to the church. It seemed... well, more respectful."

I dry my face in the handkerchief and gather my breath in sobbing gulps. "Thank you, Father. At least she was warmer there." Deep down I know how illogical my words must sound, but it is a mother's instinct to want her child to be warm.

"But to answer your question, once we laid her on the table, only then did I observe her face—at least study it, I mean. I sent Rhys to get Doctor Richards and Constable Matthews, so I had a little time alone with her."

Now it is my turn to wait. I do not wish to put words in his mouth. I want to see what comes from him without me interfering. He searches my face, pleading for help, but I remain vacant.

"She seemed peaceful, Elinor. That's all I can say. But it is the truth."

I will hold on to his words long after he has left.

CHAPTER EIGHT

There are moments when I am able to look upon what I am about to do dispassionately. During those moments, I judge my proposed action as the mark of a madwoman. But trust me when I say that a mother bereaved is willing to try anything. Anything at all. Mamgu must have believed in such things, or why else would she have written such copious notes on the subject? Therefore it is worth the risk, and besides, I have nothing to lose.

After Rowena's birth and Mamgu's death, we fled Staffordshire. I brought very little with me in the way of possessions. Truth be told, I did not own much, and most of what I did own once belonged to Mamgu. I remember the overwhelming sense of nostalgia I felt when our trunks were delivered to the cottage a few weeks later. Looking back, I do not think I grieved for Mamgu properly at the time of her death. I was so caught up in what had happened between me and Rowena's father, and with her being so young I did not have time.

But the arrival of those trunks opened the floodgates.

IMMORTELLE

Rowena's christening gown, Mamgu's bone china, and most precious of all, her collection of sketchbooks. I think I must have inherited Mamgu's artistic flair, but what she did with pencil, I do with clay. The work in the sketchbooks was so detailed and intricate, that I realized I had not taken the time or shown the interest I should have when she was alive.

I did not delve too deep at the time. It was plain to see that Mamgu's favorite subjects were flora and fauna, but the written notes which accompanied her artwork demanded time to digest, and with a young baby and a new life to establish here, I took little notice. I consoled myself that she would have been delighted because we had returned to her roots and I squirrelled her sketchbooks away.

However, a few days after Rowena's accident, I remembered and dug them out of hiding. It was Mamgu's notes and drawings that provided the ideas for Rowena's immortelle. Her notes and illustrations inspired me to choose snowdrops and a starling, but it was her written notes which led me to attempt what I am about to do tonight.

The stage is set. Visitors have long gone, and the sky is washed black as squid ink. Rowena's immortelle lies on its base, unsealed, beside the coffin. A glass dome waits, ready to enclose the miniature world, but not before her spirit has entered. Would Rowena and Mamgu condemn my actions? I hope not. I trust both of them would be willing to forgive a mother's desperate act, for I do it out of love. Neither Rowena nor I believe in God. Rowena made her feelings clear just a few weeks ago, though it feels like a lifetime. And yet we both believe that when life ends, something remains behind. All I want is to provide her an opportunity to stay close to me. To stay safe, so that whenever, if ever, she wishes to call on me, she may do so. I do not view the act as macabre, for if it works, it will be a thing of extraordinary beauty. The worst that can happen is for it to fail, and if it does, I have nothing to lose.

Despite the frosty air, the sitting room window is open, for I need to be able to hear the church clock toll at midnight. It is written that such acts of alchemy are at their most powerful during the witching hour. No one will come now. It is just me and my child, together for the last time. Tomorrow's farewell will be a public one; tonight belongs to us alone.

44

My face is pressed to the window. It cools the throbbing ache in my forehead. With all mirrors in the cottage covered, this is the first time I have seen my reflection since Rowena's accident. It is not a pretty sight. My complexion resembles a ghoul—dark circles for eyes, and my hair has grayed. I trace the fresh scar above my brow, a permanent reminder of how I collapsed on hearing the news. The eye below is purpled with bruising, and still partly closed. The bruising to my forehead has faded to a patch of sickly green. The new scar lies parallel to the old one, the one Rowena's father gave me, and is about the same length but an inch lower. The sitting room door is reflected behind me, and a mark thereon demands my attention. Two parallel lines, just like my scars, but the lines on the door frame demarcate how much Rowena grew last year. *Do you remember, Rowena, how you inched your way up the frame with each birthday? You would stretch on tippy-toes, desperate to grow up, and I would laugh and tell you to stop cheating.*

There will be no new marks. She will always remain the same height. Such things rub salt in the wounds.

The church clock strikes twelve, its first chime startling me out of my reverie. No more maudlin thoughts. It is time for action.

Once this ceremony is performed, I will say my final farewell and will never see her face again. I will close the lid on her coffin, and it will break my heart once more. But if the spell works, then it will compensate a fraction.

If Father Kendrick could see me now, he would have me condemned to a lunatic asylum, but the thought causes me no remorse. What does he know? What do any of them know? Are they any wiser because they believe they have the backing of a god? I think not. I have more faith in Mamgu's wisdom, and I shall put my trust in her, for she could always be depended on.

I light the candles, revelling in the warm glow which dances in the breeze. Inanimate things: the curtains, the drapes on Rowena's coffin, and even her shroud are animated with shadows, so it is not difficult to imagine the spell working. It fills me with hope. The shadow from the lantern flickers on the wall behind her head, hugely disproportionate in size to how it is in reality. In this room, miracles are already happening.

Mother moon has come to assist me, her full face beams

down on us. She casts a blue-tinted hue at the window, and stretches long fingers of moonbeam toward Rowena's face causing her skin to shine silver. Dark lashes do not flutter, nor does her chest rise and fall, but I know she is there. Even now, her beauty steals my breath. *You can have it, Rowena. It is yours. I would exchange my life for yours in a heartbeat.*

She lies with her face pointing east, for that is where the sun rises. To my right, sits a small pewter dish of wine, blended with oil of rosemary and six ground nuggets from the mastic tree in precise accordance with Mamgu's notes, which lie propped against the foot of the coffin. I have read the instructions over and over these past days but cannot afford to make a mistake. My hands tremble and my teeth chatter as I set light to the concoction. The cold or anxiety? I place my lips to Rowena's, a kiss as light as a feather, then take a deep breath and begin the incantation:

I command your spirit to do as I say...

Earth my body, water my blood

Air my breath and fire my spirit.
I am spirit, and I flow in you.
You are spirit, and you flow in me.

A sprinkle of soil upon her fingers, another amongst the snowdrops...

A young starling awaits your breath
It longs for your voice to give it song.
Come, Rowena, into the garden
See how it awaits your spirit.

Three starling feathers I place on her chest, six pure white snowdrops at her feet...

I command your spirit to do as I say.

The air in the room changes and stills. Even the wind outside has ceased howling. Shadows halt their dance and wait with bated breath for what might happen next. I pray in silence to all the gods—those I have no faith in, and the gods of the earth, which I do.

Inside the immortelle, the wing of the starling flutters an iridescent shimmer of purple and green. The bird blinks—just once—and the snowdrop in the center rings its tiny bell. *Ding, ding,* soft as raindrops on metal.

I hold my breath and place the glass dome on top of its base. For a fraction of a second, the smallest cloud of condensation appears inside the glass. It evaporates before I can take a breath. Did I imagine it? My face burns hot despite the cold, and mother moon comforts a stray tear with her lopsided grin.

I gaze at Rowena's body one last time, and drink in the memory of all that she is, before closing the lid of the coffin.

CHAPTER NINE

Three weeks have passed since the funeral. Three weeks of total blankness. I am devoid of emotion—the slender shell of a razor clam which has been scooped out and had its innards scattered to the wind. And the wind is enjoying the feast because each day it whistles and howls for more. But I have no more to give.

A pounding at the door makes my heart leap. The hour is late, and I am soon to retire to bed.

"Elinor, are you there?" It is Bethan's voice, I'm sure. As I open the door, a cruel gust threatens to whip her off her feet, and she grabs for her hat before it escapes. Distant calls, coming from the direction of the beach, are carried on the wind. "What is it, Bethan?"

"There's been an accident. It's the *Mary Anne*. She's been wrecked in this gale. All the villagers are down at shore doing what they can."

Without hesitation, I grab my shawl and bonnet, tying the ribbon tight beneath my chin. "Are there any survivors?"

"It doesn't appear so, though it's too soon to tell." Another gust laughs in triumph as Bethan speaks, and the branches of the holly tree groan in dismay at its callousness.

We hurry toward the beach, and frantic voices grow clearer and clearer. My pulse beats loud in my ears and saliva floods my mouth. Such events are uncommon but not unheard of in these parts, and when they occur it is the unspoken duty of all to do what they can to help.

The sky is a mass of cloud, not a star in sight, and the rain lashes against our skin as we battle ever onward. Neither of us has the breath to speak, and in any case, we would be unlikely to hear one another in this wind.

The sea roars with anger. She pounds the rocky shore, spitting spray high into the air. The beach is strewn with a variety of shapes, some moving, others still. It is impossible to recognize anyone in particular since they are all black silhouettes.

A pitiful sight. The *Mary Anne* lies on her side close to the jutting rocks which have tripped her up. She is torn down the middle, great wooden ribs bared and bleeding, though her innards ooze foamy water, not blood. Her mast has been snapped in two and remnants of white sail cloth frantically wave for attention. From all around comes sighing and groaning, though it is impossible to discriminate between the moans of humans and those of the damaged sloop.

Barrels bob in the sea, two of which are draped with bodies that cling like barnacles in their attempt to use them as float aids. But the wrathful sea has a different idea and instead of bringing the sailors closer to shore, it carries them further out in its ebbing current. Rescuers, thigh deep in foaming waves, try their best to gain progress, but the ocean is enjoying the thrill of the chase and is unwilling to relinquish its contraband.

For several moments I stand rooted, taking in the scene around me and wondering how I might help. And then I see the figure on the sand. Just a few feet away lies a body facedown. Why is no one attending to him? I find my feet and run. Heaving with all my might, I attempt to turn him over. Now I understand the true meaning of dead weight. *Is this how Rhys felt when he lifted Rowena?* I push the thought from my mind. I must try and help the man or I will never forgive myself.

Eventually, after several attempts, his body succumbs to my

49

efforts and he flops, without grace, onto his back. If I had to guess, I would estimate his age to be around forty, though it is difficult to tell in such poor light. I call for help, but my shout is snatched by the wind. I am muted. Tilting his head to the side, I watch as a stream of water drains from his mouth and nose, and I cannot stop my thoughts turning to Rowena. I fight the urge to flee.

The stream of water stops, so I turn him to face me. His eyes are closed, so he cannot witness the despair on my face. I pinch his nostrils, my fingers slippery and numb with cold, then cover his lips with mine. Four strong breaths that urge him to live, followed by four pumps to the heart with the heels of my hands. *Don't give up!* But despite my repeated efforts, it is too late. I am too late. I do not know if I am crying, because my face is already soaked with rain. I rise to my feet, tilt my head toward the heavens, and scream with frustration.

A little in the distance, another man sits on the sand. His head is in his hands and he rocks gently, as if he cannot bear to watch. He wears the same oilskin and boots as the dead man, so I assume he too must be from the wreck. I am filled with joy to see at least one survivor. I lift my skirts and run toward him, wanting to offer words of comfort. He lifts his head, notices my approach, and then I see it. Not only does he wear the same garments as the dead man, but he has the exact same features—a mop of graying hair stuck fast to his skin, bushy eyebrows, and a sharp chin. I stop in my tracks. *A twin?* He looks at me and smiles, but not with his eyes. Then, like a footprint in the sand, he fades to nothing.

Morning dawns with a flush of pink, repentant for the previous night's gale. The middle of March and now, instead of snowdrops, the banks are filled with daffodils. Their bright, cheerful faces smile in relief because the storm is over. If they could, they would trumpet a bugle call as a mark of respect for those lost in the wreck.

On my way to the graveyard, I am tempted to pick a few daffodils, but I resist. Rowena preferred to see them growing in the earth rather than kept alive by artificial means in a vase of water. I have so much to tell her today. I am glad she did not have to witness the storm. It would have upset her to see such sights on the beach. Mother nature can be so cruel at times.

Every day I visit her place of rest. Every day I hope to hear the snowdrop or see the starling flutter its wings. Most of all I hope to hear its voice, but of course my hopes are not realized. Today, though, my faith in the afterlife is renewed, for last night I saw a ghost.

I kneel on the damp grass beside her grave and talk to her as I always do. "Do you remember asking if I had ever seen a ghost and me telling you about the night my mother died, and about how she came to me briefly and sat at the bottom of my bed?" My voice is a whisper, and all the while I watch the immortelle for any sign of movement. "As I said at the time, it never happened again. Until last night at the beach. The encounter was fleeting, no more than an acknowledgement, but it fills me with hope that one day your ghost might come to me."

My words fall on deaf ears, but I will persist.

Rowena's immortelle is admired by all. So many from the village have complimented me on it, though none of them know the meaning behind my choices, nor do they have the slightest inclination as to the alchemy involved the night before her funeral. It is our secret and will remain so.

I made a promise to myself this morning: I shall begin to sort through her belongings. Witnessing the ghost last night has spurred me on. Her bedroom remains exactly as it did on the day of her accident, and while I cannot part with any of her belongings, I need, at least, to freshen the room. Once I have finished here, I intend to give it a clean, and tidy away her muddles. She always was an untidy little devil. We fought over the state of her room, but I would give my right arm to do the same now.

I say my goodbyes and promise to return tomorrow and to let her know how I coped. I tell her not to worry, reassuring her I will not pry into her personal belongings. She was on the verge of becoming a woman and deserves some privacy.

Rowena's robin is waiting for me on the gatepost when I return. He misses her, too. She was so patient and kind, and had him eating out of her hand. He doesn't yet trust me to the same degree, but I am working on it.

I am about to start on Rowena's room when there is a knock at the door. I am surprised to find Gwyneth standing there, as she is usually busy at the farm at this time of day. I am glad for the disruption because now that I am home, I am less inclined to tackle the task I had planned.

"I've come with a message, bach," she says, shouldering her way inside with blatant familiarity. Gwyneth and I have become good friends since Rowena's death. She is like a second mother to me now. Having shared an experience so personal, so emotional as the laying out of one's child, any assumed barrier has been broken. In her hands she carries a tin. I have no doubt other than it will be full of Welsh cakes. She is always trying to tempt my appetite, and I do not have the heart to tell her I despise dried fruit. She plonks the tin down on the kitchen table. "Is the kettle on?" she asks. "I'm gasping for a cuppa."

I smile to myself. "What message, Gwyneth?" She seems to have forgotten her purpose.

"Oh, yes, from the wife of Captain Thomas. She wants to know if you're willing to make an immortelle for his grave."

It comes as a shock. I have not considered making another. "I don't know, Gwyneth. I've not given it any thought."

"She'll pay well. The family is wealthy, bach. You could do with an extra shilling or two in the coffers, I'm sure."

I mash the tea, considering the offer. "Tell her to come and see me. We can talk about what she wants in person."

"Rightio, bach. I'm popping up to the big house later to pay my respects. She and I have known one another since we were kids. I imagine she's taking it hard. Losing him to the storm last night will have come as a dreadful shock."

"I'm sure it will have. And what about the other sailors, Gwyn? Were they all locals?" I can't help but think about the man I tried to save... and his ghost. It is hard to believe all this happened just one night ago.

"Guess so. Expect I'll know more later when I visit."

We make small talk, avoiding the more gruesome detail of the previous night. My guess is she does not want to upset me, not with so much drowning. But my mind is on other things, for already I am planning Captain Thomas's immortelle. Perhaps a replica of the *Mary Anne*, or some other symbol of the sea? A riot of color with kelp, anemones, and starfish. My breath shudders with excitement. I must not let my imagination run away with me. Perhaps Mrs Thomas will not want to be reminded of his life at sea.

Gwyneth's invitation has renewed my resolve to tackle Rowena's room, but before I begin, I lie on her bed, as I have done on many occasions these past weeks. Her scent is fading. Only the faintest trace of warm rosemary and lime lingers, and it saddens me. I remember how I would hold her close, breathe in the scent of her hair. A knotted fist forms in my throat, threatening to choke me. I open the window wide and allow the cool spring air to steal the remains of Rowena's scent. And know what I must do.

It is as I remove the bottom sheet that I see it: a book, hidden between mattress and bed frame. My heart somersaults. The book lies face down, and when I turn it over, I see it is a copy of *The Lancashire Witches* by William Harrison Ainsworth. I have a vague memory of having read it many years ago. My first thought is that such a novel would not be appropriate for someone of Rowena's age, and perhaps that is why she saw fit to hide it. A sliver of red ribbon lies at page forty-three. I assume this is as far as she read. I am torn. Torn between wondering who might have loaned her such a text and at the same time filled with sadness because she will never get to finish it.

Was this another of her secrets? Or is it linked somehow to her death? I bundle the sheets and place the book on top of the pile, but it slides to the floor, falling open at a different page, a page which bears an altogether different place marker. I bend down to pick it up. It is an envelope, addressed to no other than Father Kendrick. My hands tremble as I turn it over. The envelope is empty and postmarked several months earlier. Did Father Kendrick loan her the book? Surely not. But how else did it come to be in her possession?

CHAPTER TEN

Throughout the night I am a tempest, tossing and turning, unable to focus on anything other than the book. It makes no sense. Rowena had made her dislike of Father Kendrick clear, so I cannot imagine her having anything to do with him outside of church. My thoughts slip from innocent coincidence to violent mistrust and back again so many times that come dawn, I am exhausted.

There is only one way to find out; I must tackle him head on. I consider myself highly intuitive, so I shall be able to sense if he lies.

It takes little in the way of courage to prepare myself for the visit to The Rectory, for I cannot wait. Rowena's robin follows me all the way down the lane, though I need no chaperone. The book and envelope are concealed in the pocket of my dress, and I am ready to do battle.

At first, I am a little taken aback when he opens the door unshaven and dressed in an open-necked shirt. Never before have

I seen him out of vestments. He seems just as surprised by my dishevelled appearance and takes a step back, frowning.

"May I come in, Father?"

He hesitates, then thinks better of it. "Of course, Elinor. Whatever is the matter?"

I say nothing as I step inside. My hands are trembling, which annoys me, as I wish to appear in control. He shows me into the sitting room. It is stark—the room of a single man. No fire is lit and there is very little in the way of ornamentation. The room is not dirty, and yet the air carries a musty smell.

"Excuse my state of dress, Elinor, but I haven't long risen. What time is it?"

I have not considered the time and realize with a modicum of embarrassment that it is around eight-thirty. Too early for a social call. "I couldn't sleep, Father. I have things on my mind."

He chews his bottom lip. "Please, take a seat. Can I get you some tea?" I am sure his voice falters a little and he has paled, but perhaps I imagine it. I refuse his offer of tea. I do not wish to give him time to come up with excuses. By now, if he is guilty, he must realize I have uncovered something.

A quick scan of the room offers a sagging sofa, close to threadbare, and two wooden captain's chairs. I choose the one nearest to me and hope he will choose the sofa. I would prefer to look down on him when I ask about the book and envelope. Instead he stands, and leans an arm against the mantelpiece, playing me at my own game.

"So how might I help you?"

I cut to the chase. "Did Rowena ever visit you, Father?"

He takes a deep breath. "What do you mean, visit?"

"I mean here, outside of church?" My nerves are steel. The evidence remains hidden from sight. A strong beam of sunlight shines through the front window, revealing beads of sweat on his upper lip. Once again Mother Nature has proven she is on my side.

"Well, we would sometimes speak as she passed by on her way home from school, but then you know that since I gave her a basket of apples." He shakes his head, and narrows his eyes. "Why do you ask such a thing?"

I slide the book from my pocket, slippery as a dagger. "Did you give her this?"

He frowns, takes a step closer and peers at the title as if he has never seen it before. "*The Lancashire Witches*. Of course not! Whyever would you think such a thing?"

All the time I am judging him, as he so often does others. "Are you certain?" I fail to give him his title, and the gesture is intentional. My hand returns to my pocket and from it I pluck the envelope, holding it in front of his face so that he can read his name. "Then how did *this* happen to be inside the book?"

He takes the envelope from me, and examines it closely. "Listen, Elinor," his voice trembles. Spittle foams at the corner of his mouth, "if you are suggesting anything inappropriate—"

I cut him off, hearing the pitch of my own voice rising. "Then explain it. How else would an envelope addressed to you be inside the book she happened to be reading?"

"Where did you find it?" He is floundering—doggy-paddling, and getting nowhere.

"In Rowena's bedroom, concealed beneath the mattress." I have the upper hand and he knows it.

"Look. I have never seen that book before and have no idea why Rowena should have an envelope addressed to me in her possession. Might I suggest it is just a coincidence, and that in your grief you are putting two and two together and making five?"

I steady my nerves, and swallow my ferocity. "No, Father, you may not. I told you when you visited the night before the funeral. I will not give up until I have answers." I point my finger close to his face. "Do not underestimate the wrath of a mother."

He waves the envelope in the air as if he wishes it would fly away. "Perhaps she picked the envelope up at church and used it as a book marker."

Do I imagine the desperation in his eyes? "Her page was marked with the ribbon. The envelope was further along and fell to the floor as I picked up the book."

"Come now, Elinor," he scoffs, and it is all I can do to stop myself from reaching for his throat. "How do you know which page she read to? For goodness sake!"

My mouth falls open. I have not considered this. The envelope might well have marked her page, not the ribbon, but it does not alter the fact that it once belonged to him and I tell him so.

He stops waving and brings the offensive object to his nose.

"Let me take a better look, see if I can identify the handwriting." He squints at the envelope and the tension in his shoulders eases. "I thought as much. It is Father Michael's handwriting. See for yourself." He strides toward a desk, slides out a drawer, and rummages through the contents. "Here," he says, waving a similar envelope at me. "He sent this one to me just before I took over the position." He slips out a letter, and stabs at Father Michael's signature.

I take a deep breath. My strength is wavering. "Even so, it still does not explain why Rowena had the other one in her possession, does it?"

He grins, a smug look on his face. "In actual fact it does. I distinctly remember the letter you speak of arriving just as I was leaving for church one morning, and therefore I took it with me. Father Michael had written to ask how I was settling in. The letter is in my desk in the vestry. In fact, I saw it there just a week or so ago. I remember thinking it strange because the envelope was missing, but I assumed I must have binned it. It's quite obvious that Rowena had taken it." He pauses for breath. "Come to the church with me now if you like. I will show you."

His manner is self-assured, though a little angry, and I find myself faltering. "Whether or not you read the letter at home or at the church does not explain how it came to be in Rowena's possession. The suggestion is ridiculous!"

He pauses and shifts his feet before dropping the bombshell. "Ah, but it isn't. I'm sorry to tell you, Elinor, but Rowena was not as innocent as you like to think."

"How do you mean?" My anger is rising. How dare he!

"Think back to twelfth night. If you remember, you and Delyth were packing away the Christmas decorations."

I nod, wondering where this is leading.

"I arrived late. You and Delyth were packing boxes while Sioned sat beside you chewing toffee. I distinctly remember asking her where she had found the toffee and her getting flustered."

I nod, remembering precisely the moment of which he speaks. "I remember, but what does that have to do with the envelope?"

"Where was Rowena?"

I flounder, for I cannot remember her being there. Minutes earlier Delyth and I had sent the girls into the vestry with the boxes but Sioned returned alone. "I–I cannot say."

"Well I am sorry to tell you, Elinor, Rowena was in the vestry going through my things."

I gasp. I cannot deny that Rowena was a curious child, defiant at times. "But—"

"She had taken the key to the desk from my cassock pocket and had unlocked it. I found her rummaging among the contents."

I am lost for words, unsure of whether to apologize or press on with my accusation. I need time to think about what he has said. My body slumps, the wind has been knocked from my sails.

"I wouldn't have told you, Elinor, not unless—"

My lip trembles. "Then I am sorry, Father. Forgive me." I get to my feet, realizing I still have the book in my hand. Not the envelope, though. It has found its way back to its master.

"Think nothing of it... look, I understand how difficult it must be for you. You feel you need answers, but they are not forthcoming. This is all part of grief, Elinor. Listen, we shall say no more about it, all right?"

As I stumble my way toward the cottage, I see Gwyneth waiting at the gate. "Thought you wouldn't be gone long," she says. "Got a bit of news for you." Then she sees my face and knows something is wrong. "What's up, bach? You look as if you've seen a ghost."

I am grateful for her company and I decide then and there to tell her what has happened. I need to confide in someone, and she is the one person I trust enough to discuss such things with.

"I'll speak candidly," she says when I tell her what has happened. "If I were you, I'd let it go. I'm not overly keen on Father Kendrick either, but I don't think he'd mess about with a child." She shakes her head and emits a kind of *neigh*. Spent too much time amongst animals, I think, feeling somewhat cheered by her response. Perhaps I have been overly hasty. "You know how kids Rowena's age are. Inquisitive little buggers, and if they think they shouldn't have something they want it all the more. I wouldn't mind betting one of her classmates loaned her the book."

"But the envelope, Gwyn. It still doesn't sit right with me."

"Well, is what he said true? Did Rowena go missing when you and Delyth were packing the boxes?"

"Yes, Gwyn. We sent the two girls to the vestry, but Rowena didn't come back, at least not for a while."

"There you are. Think back, now. Try to remember how Rowena seemed when she did return."

I close my eyes and focus. It's difficult to remember, with all that has happened. One minute she was missing, the next she was there, but come to think of it, she had seemed a bit sullen. I put it down to boredom or because Sioned had taken the last of the toffee. "You know, Gwyn, she did seem a bit suspicious, and I wouldn't put it past her if I'm honest. She was always so bloody curious." The memory stings.

"Well there you have it. I bet he caught her red-handed. You said she preferred Father Michael, didn't you? She was probably reading his letter when Father Kendrick came in and she tried to hide the fact by slipping the envelope in her pocket. I mean, she'd hardly have had time to put the letter back in the envelope, would she?"

It comes as a relief in a way. Maybe I am still harboring negative thoughts about Father Kendrick because he was there when Rowena died and I was not.

I pour the tea, chewing over Gwyneth's words in my mind. "Thanks, Gwyn. I feel a bit better."

"That's all right, bach, you know I'm here for you. Oh, by the way, Mrs. Thomas asked if you can visit her on Thursday, you know, to discuss the immortelle." She chuckles, and the gap in her front teeth reminds me of Chaucer's "Wife of Bath," though somehow I do not imagine Gwyneth to be of a similar disposition. "You know how wealthy folk are—they'd rather us do the running-about than the other way round."

CHAPTER ELEVEN

Captain Thomas's house stands on the cliff top overlooking the sea, and I am breathless by the time I arrive. Breathless because of the steep incline, and breathless because the house is far more imposing than I imagined. I would not have considered the owner of a few herring boats to be so wealthy, but then I should have known better, as nearby Aberporth is one of the most important herring trade ports in the whole of the country.

The house is built of stone, triple-gabled, and commands a spectacular view of the Irish Sea. I am overwhelmed by its proportions and cannot help but feel great sadness to think the captain will never see it again.

It is likely he lies in repose within, and I am suddenly afraid Mrs. Thomas might expect me to pay my respects. I am acquainted with both the Thomas's through church but know neither of them personally, and I am not of the mind to see another dead body just yet.

The door is answered by Jenny, the housekeeper, who I also

know from church. As a visitor to the wife of the deceased I am dressed in black as a mark of respect, as is Jenny. She shows me into the parlour, which is lamplit despite the fact that it is ten o'clock in the morning. Since the curtains remain drawn, in accordance with tradition, it is to be expected.

The room is elegantly furnished in reds and gold, and a fire roars in the ornate fireplace; it is a welcome addition on such a cold day. It is late March, and winter and spring are engaged in battle, though there is no doubt spring will be the victor.

The distinct aroma of pipe tobacco hangs in the air. It will fade soon, what with the captain gone. Jenny takes my cloak and gloves, and invites me to take a seat. The room is extraordinarily silent, morbidly so, and I realize it is because even the grandfather clock has been stopped.

A minute or so later, Mrs. Thomas sweeps into the room, her long hair in a severe bun and her face blotchy with grief. I stand as she enters, and she takes my cold hand in hers. Her grasp is weak, and she trembles. "Thank you for coming," she says, and her welcome seems so genuine that any anxiety I feel melts away. "I thought perhaps you might not want to do it, not with your little one gone so short a time ago."

I take a deep breath and swallow the lump that rises in my throat. "To be honest, Mrs. Thomas, I did not imagine making another immortelle, but I am happy to do so. I must say how sorry I am for your loss. Captain Thomas will be sorely missed in these parts, and the *Mary Anne* brought employment to many locals."

Her chin quivers at my words. "I think I'm still in shock, but you will know all about that, so forgive me if I seem a little distracted at times."

Jenny returns with a tray of tea and we discuss Rowena's immortelle.

"Of course I knew such things were becoming popular around the country, but I have never seen one quite like your daughter's," Mrs. Thomas says.

"You're right, Mrs. Thomas. Immortelles are usually provided by the funeral director and as such are generic in design. I believe they have been popular in France for quite some time. You know how we British are; it takes us a while before we end up imitating our continental cousins."

She manages a smile and the lines on her face relax.

"So, do you have any particular design in mind?" I ask, hoping she will not be too specific so that my imagination is free to run wild.

"Something to do with the sea, of course, but I don't think it should include the *Mary Anne*, at least not in name. The cutter was named after our daughter, you see, and I wouldn't want it upsetting her every time she visits her father's grave."

"That's perfectly understandable, but do you want a boat of any kind included, or would you rather something more abstract?"

"No, no, perhaps a model of a cutter, but without a name." She sips her tea and her eyes water. I know for certain she has slipped back into the past.

"Then how about you tell me a bit about Captain Thomas, you know, the kind of man he was, not his public persona, and I will listen. Your information will help me choose the most suitable memorial."

She puts down her cup, sighs, and spins a yarn of young love, and the sea, the birth of their daughter, and growing old together. And all the while the scent of pipe tobacco, old leather, and the ocean fills the air.

Captain Thomas hears. I am certain of it.

I run my fingers over the mark on the door frame, the place we last measured Rowena's height. It is level with the bottom of my chin. She was tall for her age. I close my eyes and try to picture the crown of her head tucked into my neck when last I hugged her but fail to do so. Those last few months she was reluctant to make physical contact and would pull away if I tried to hug her. Today she would have turned twelve, and all I can give her is a bunch of yellow daffodils.

Spring is winning the battle today. The air is magnolia-scented, and as I walk down the lane the bleat of newborn lambs carries from the fields surrounding the church. I cannot help but be cheered. A child's birthday makes any mother nostalgic. One cannot help but revisit the birth and the formative years, but when the child is no longer present the feeling is thrice-fold.

As I enter the graveyard my stomach drops, for I catch sight of Father Kendrick leaving the church. What is he doing here at this time of morning? I thought I knew his routine well enough to avoid him. He has spotted me, though, so I cannot.

"Glorious morning," he says, with a nod toward the sky. "Daffodils today, I see. You do not usually bring flowers."

I stumble over my words. "It's Rowena's birthday, Father. She would have been twelve today."

His face falls. "I'm sorry, Elinor. Today must be very difficult for you."

"Every day is difficult, Father. Not just today." I feel a little embarrassed about our last meeting. Maybe I owe him an apology. "Father, the other day, I—"

He raises a hand in protest. "I thought we agreed to say no more about it."

I nod, grateful for his understanding, though I still cannot say I trust him. My intuition tells me something is amiss with the man. Then, before I can stop myself, I say, "Oh, by the way, Father, Captain Thomas's wife has asked me to make an immortelle in preparation for his funeral."

It seems he has already been told because he shows no hint of surprise. Instead he says, "How wonderful. Will you let me know when it's finished? I would like to see it."

My instinct is to be rude and tell him how he has changed his tune since labelling Rowena's immortelle frivolous, but I bite my tongue. Maybe my talent being acknowledged by the wealthy has helped change his mind. "I will, Father. I imagine the funeral will be attended by many."

"Indeed. Now I'll let you get on and visit your daughter." Then, as I am about to walk away, he says, "God knows this is the day of her birth, Elinor. You can be certain."

As I kneel at the graveside the first thing I do is apologize. "I know you do not approve of cut flowers, Rowena, but what else can I bring you?"

The rest of our conversation, though really it cannot be classed as such since it is one-directional, is carried out in silence. I tell her about my ideas for the captain's immortelle, about how grand the Thomas's house is, but I do not mention the book or envelope. I do not want to upset her on her birthday.

When I return to the cottage, I feel the need to distract myself from an overwhelming sense of loss, so I spend the rest of the day in the pottery. Captain Thomas is to be buried in four days' time, which does not give me long to complete his immortelle.

I am certain both Captain Thomas and his wife would prefer a traditional memorial: one which speaks of his life at sea but also hints at the kind gentleman he was, for his reputation as a good master and a loving father and husband goes before him.

The model of the clipper is prepared and ready to glaze, as is the rocky base. I have included a miniature compass to help the captain find his way home however far he sails. There is no need to model such things as shells as I have the real thing within my vast collection. Which to choose? I know the Thomas's are God-fearing people, so my decision must respect their belief.

The scallop shell is often used as a vessel from which to sprinkle baptism water. It will make a nice touch, as will the inclusion of pearl since, according to Revelations, the twelve gates of heaven were made from a single pearl. I doubt whether Father Kendrick or Mrs. Thomas will have any understanding of the other associations with pearl. According to Mamgu's notes, pearl is representative of moonlight and tears, wealth, and the power of the waters, which to my mind seem far more apt.

And sea creatures, too. The crab, which scurries sideways, proving one's life does not always follow a straight path. Miniature starfish, which I will glaze ochre and finish with rows of tiny turquoise beads will contrast the natural tones well. Mamgu's words make so much sense when I think about them. Of course, the starfish is able to regenerate its limbs, or even its entire body—what better symbol of resurrection could there be?

I am in my element, the gaping hole that is the loss of Rowena temporarily plugged with clay. My art is the one thing which distracts me from my grief. As I arrange the limbs of the starfish my mind drifts back to the night of the storm and the image of the sailor on the beach—the man I tried to help. I suppose it is the five-pronged shape, like the head and limbs of the body splayed on the sand.

Gwyneth confirmed that every man who lost his life had lived within a few miles of here, though there has been no mention of another funeral at Eglwys y Grog, so I assume they were not from our village.

The crab's antennae are fixed in place and I am about to insert its eyes when I sense it. For a moment I believe I have entered the soul of the crab and am seeing through its eyes, those light-sensitive facets on each stalk which enable it to see three-hundred-and-sixty degrees. The light has dimmed, just a fraction, and with it comes a sudden chill. The hairs on the back of my neck stand on end and I shiver. My fingers are motionless, my breath captive, and as I turn, a plume of pipe smoke wafts toward me. I taste it on my tongue—complicated, aromatic, and with just a hint of burnt cherry.

Captain Thomas has come to see how I am doing.

CHAPTER TWELVE

As I have already said, it is the nights that are the worst. By day I am able to distract my thoughts to some degree through my art, but once I leave the pottery, the wound re-opens. It trickles a trail from my heart into my stomach until I am barely able to function. I know Rowena would not want this. She would hate to see me destroyed, but I am unable to heal.

Some nights I stay in the pottery until long past midnight. It is almost as if I am afraid of the cottage. There are so many memories of Rowena there, and while I want to remember her, I tend to focus on the bad times. Those last few weeks when she was not herself come back to haunt me. Why did I not persist in discovering what ailed her? Worst of all is the guilt. Friends tell me guilt is part of grieving and I must not blame myself, but how can I not?

I will never know for certain whether she administered the poison herself or whether someone else is to blame. I will never know her final thoughts, and I am consumed by the thought of her fear. The coroner believes the poison made her sick, disorientated, and as a result she accidentally drowned in the trough, but it is all supposition.

I am as tormented as St. Anthony in Schongauer's engraving, but whereas he calmly resists the demons' blows, I fail to resist mine, for they are of my own making.

I lie on Rowena's bed, attempting to read *The Lancashire Witches*. At least I can imagine Rowena's thoughts as she read it. Perhaps it will bring me closer to her and might even invoke a sense of my own witchcraft because, as hard as I tried the night before her funeral, it seems as if my success was imagined. I do not doubt I saw the ghost of the sailor, and Captain Thomas, too. So how am I able to sense the presence of both men but not my own child?

The introduction to *The Lancashire Witches* is long-winded. It consists of several chapters which provide historical background to the story. Vague recollections return as I read, and in particular I remember how I struggled to read the parts written in dialect. I imagine Rowena must have struggled, too. She would have enjoyed the story, though, especially the part where the abbot curses the witch and her infant. Perhaps I was wrong in imagining Father Kendrick gave the book to her. It does not portray established religion in a good light, and I cannot help but smile knowing she would have enjoyed that particular aspect.

I read as far as the ribboned marker. Did Rowena stop here? If so, she will never discover what happened to Jennet, the small, deformed girl with cunning features, nor will she learn of Alice Nutter, an English woman accused and hanged as a result of the Pendle witch hunt. Such terrible times, though some would still carry out such crimes against women today if they could get away with it.

Planet Mercury winks at the window. Mercury—the messenger god. He has come to tell me there is a way for Rowena to finish the story. Of course! I will read to her at the graveside, a few chapters every day, though I hope she will not laugh at my dire attempt at a Lancashire accent. The thought cheers me a little.

I have not seen Rowena's robin for a few days, not even when I scatter cake or bread around the porch. I hope it is because summer is approaching, and he prefers to forage in the woods rather than beg for food in the garden. I do not like to think he has gone because she is no longer here.

Since Captain Thomas's funeral, I have been inundated with requests for immortelles. Word has spread throughout the county it seems, and while I do not wish to turn work down, I fear I must, as each immortelle is labour intensive. It is their individuality that prevents me from agreeing to every request. If I were to take on every project, I would be unable to carry out other ceramic work, such as the studio ceramics which I have been enjoying. Therefore, I have decided to prioritize requests from locals and will agree to those from further afield if time permits.

Rowena would be proud of me. Who would have thought I would become famous for making memorials for the dead?

It is a glorious day. The lambs in the field have grown confident. They play with their siblings in an amusing fashion, each trying to outdo the other when it comes to seeing who can jump highest. I cannot help but smile at their sheer joy.

As I kneel at Rowena's grave, the ocean laps at the cliffs and hungry gulls squabble over scraps. Today I shall feed them a diet of words. I hope they will receive some nourishment, though I am certain they would prefer herring.

I am unsure where to start, Rowena. At the ribboned marker or the page which once contained Father Kendrick's envelope? My gut instinct tells me you read as far as the ribbon marker, so we shall begin there.

I read of the May Day maypole, of Alizon the beautiful May Queen and her sister Jennet's jealousy. I explain its roots in Paganism and how the established church frowned upon such festivities. The rebellious side of me, the side which still harbours doubts about Father Kendrick, wishes he would appear. Perhaps he too would like a lesson in Paganism.

I wish you had not hidden the book from me, Rowena. Although I still consider it a little macabre for someone your age, we could have read it together, as we do now.

I finish another chapter and my thoughts return to pessimism. *What else did you hide from me, Rowena? I wish you could give me a sign, an indication you are still with me. It is all I will ever want.*

I must try harder to pluck myself out of this melancholy. I do not want her to see me grieve like this, but I cannot help it. One minute, I am sane and focused on the task in hand—the next, I am thrown into turmoil. I cannot imagine such angst will ever truly subside.

What do you think of Captain Thomas's immortelle, Rowena? I imagine you approve of the starfish and crab and the little fishing boat. Do you remember how we would scour the beach looking for treasure? Why did we stop? Was it because you were growing up, or was there a more sinister reason for your sudden disinterest in such things?

I shall have to say goodbye for now. There is a new glaze I am experimenting with, a pale plum, opalescent finish using cadmium and selenium. As well you know, Rowena, red glazes can often be an ordeal by fire. The test tile is ready to be unloaded from the kiln and I am eager to see the results. If it is successful, I shall bring it with me when I visit you tomorrow, and you shall have a lesson in chemistry and a lesson in witchcraft, both in one day.

Today I wake to the same sickening sense of loss I have felt over these past few months: a complete sense of shock and denial as consciousness takes over. But once I am fully awake, the thought of reading further chapters to Rowena motivates me to get out of bed.

The Lancashire Witches rests in one pocket of my dress, a pink-glazed test tile in the other. I am pleased with the result and look forward to showing it to her.

The breeze from the sea is feisty this morning. It gusts at my back, urging me toward the grave as though it cannot wait for me to get there. And when I reach it, I see the reason for its excitement. Sitting on top of Rowena's immortelle is a shell. Its position is not haphazard but has been placed dead centre. My heart beats rapidly. Who could have put it there?

On closer examination I see it is a bivalve, a small clam-like shell, smooth and delicate with striated growth bands. The color is most striking, for such shells are most often pale yellow or dusky pink, like a fading rose. This one is not. It is deeper in color, almost plum-toned. And then I remember the tile. I slip it from my pocket, and hold it against the shell with trembling fingers. It's not a perfect match, but almost. Mere coincidence, or is it a gift from Rowena? It must be, she was the only one who knew about my glazing experiment. My heart glows, full of hope. This is the most promising sign yet that she is still with me.

How to begin? I am breathless. My voice quivers as I attempt to read the next chapter, but I will plough on because it is what I have come here to do. Some of my most precious memories are of the two of us telling stories. She was a quick learner and had mastered the basics of reading by the age of five.

Today I read of an infant, thrown into fire in a fit of spite, a ghostly monk appearing from behind a wall hanging, and perhaps most sinister of all, a gathering of witches at a ruined church who call on the help of a demon from the bowels of the earth.

I trust all this talk of demons and witches will not steal into her dreams. I am guilty of far greater negligence. Guilty of not insisting she told me what irked her. Guilty of failing to notice her late return from school. And worst of all, guilty of not being able to solve the puzzle of what happened on the day she was taken from me.

But she has provided me with a gift today, and I shall hold it close and allow it to give me strength to go forward.

PART THREE

CHAPTER THIRTEEN

More than a year has passed since Rowena's death. They say time heals. It is a myth. Time cements one's grief into an impregnable slab of rock. It hardens you to the degree that things which once touched you or brought you joy are no longer felt. Denial, anger, plea bargaining—the whole gamut of emotion dissipates along with hope, serenity, and pride, until all one is left with is blank acceptance and love. Love never dies.

Little has changed hereabouts. Babies are born and people die, just as they do the world over.

If you were to have visited the churchyard at Eglwys y Grog while Rowena was still here, you would have seen nothing re-markable—just a white-washed church beside the sea, and a graveyard dotted with the same slabs of gray as any other. Now my immortelles attract visitors from miles away. When she feels so inclined, the sun shines down on their glass domes, spotlight-ing individual arrangements like actors on the stage. I am told strangers like to view the displays and piece together clues about the kind of life the deceased once lived.

What was once a dour, gray-slabbed space has been transformed into a cacophony of color, full of miniature birds and sea creatures, flowers and farm-implements, which, from afar, give the impression of a Kingdom of the Fae.

There is so much call for my work, and each piece takes so much time to perfect, that I am rarely able to complete it in readiness for the funeral. This has come to be accepted by those bereaved, preferred even. The graves of those recently buried are adorned with fresh flowers and wreaths, and as soon as the fresh flowers die, they are replaced with an immortelle: a permanent and personal memorial to those who have been lost.

I am still not certain as to whether or not Father Kendrick approves of my work, though he seems almost obsessed with it, taking the time to visit me at the pottery whenever he knows a new immortelle has been made, where he proceeds to pass judgement over the piece as though he were himself a master craftsman.

After all this time I am still not enamoured with the man, and aside from his brief visits, have very little to do with him. I do my best to avoid him at church, and if I see him walking the coast path or the beach, I scurry away like a mouse from a cat.

His sermons have been tinged with darkness of late, as has his expression, and he often seems lost in his own world. Last Sunday he preached from the book of Samuel, rejoicing in King Saul's request to the Witch of Endor where she summons a spirit from the dead.

The previous week his black eyes glinted like coals when he spoke of King Belshazzar's encounter with a disembodied hand, which wrote the words *mene, mene, teqel, parsin* on the wall, thus predicting the King's demise.

On another occasion he grew quite animated whilst reading from the book of Mark and told us the story of Christ as he cast out a legion of demons from a man living in a graveyard. His words made me shiver with unease because the cliffside setting of the story was so similar to ours. His voice echoed to the rafters when the story reached its climax and the host of demons, cast out of the man, instead entered a drove of pigs which charged down the cliff and were drowned.

I cannot help but think how Rowena would have enjoyed

such stories. She hated being forced to attend church; perhaps such tales would have proved more agreeable.

Each day I visit her grave, there is something to tell her, some snippet of news or words of gossip. Since finishing *The Lancashire Witches,* we have shared many other stories, most of which have their roots in something other than Christianity. I suppose I am rebellious in nature, reading such things on sacred ground. I admit she inherited the trait from me.

I tell her about my work, the immortelles and studio ceramics. I explain what I have discovered in Mamgu's writing and tell of her illustrative talent. I speak of babies born, old folk who are sick, and how the whole village is devastated by the news that Mari Howell has died from pneumonia. Such a waste. The life of one so gifted, cut short in its prime. Mari's immortelle required much consideration. She was so well thought of in these parts, indeed throughout the country, and I needed to choose things suited to a life of music and song.

Her grave lies just behind Rowena's. Her immortelle includes the bay laurel—the symbol of honour and fame—and the bluebell—symbolic of sorrowful regret, for on the day of her funeral there was not a dry eye in the church.

Something strange happened the day of Mari's funeral, something that has given me hope. As we trooped from church with our heads bowed low and damp handkerchiefs clasped tight in our fists, a shrill tweet broke the silence. I lifted my head to see a young starling sat atop Rowena's headstone. The shock of seeing it made me tremble, and from that moment on, Father Kendrick's words of sorrow were lost to me. The starling remained for the whole proceeding, though respectfully it stayed silent until the committal was over. I cannot help but think it was Rowena's way of paying her respect to Mari.

And I have seen it many times since. Though shy at first, it soon gained confidence and now waits for me in front of the porch and follows me down the lane toward the church, playing hide-and-go-seek with the trees which border the lane, before racing across the field to meet me at the lych-gate. It trills the sweetest song, though I am yet to hear it speak in Rowena's voice.

I remain hopeful that one day she will come to let me know she is here. Whether it be through the voice of the starling or in the form of a ghost, I do not care. But I do know this—if I am able to see the ghosts of those I did not know or barely knew in life, the phenomena of the afterlife is proven.

From my studies I have learned the spirits of those we lose are the ones which make such choices, not us. There are many reasons why a soul might not wish to make its presence known, and after careful consideration, I have concluded that Rowena stays away to keep me safe. She knows that should I ever discover someone else was involved in her death, I would not be able to prevent myself from wreaking revenge. She also knows she cannot make herself known to me without breaking such a confidence. This, I am convinced, is the reason she stays away.

Time has passed by in a haze. Sometimes there seems a twinkle of light at the end of the tunnel, and at other times the future remains dark. It is my friends who keep me going, Gwyneth in particular, but most of all it is my work with pottery. The focus provided by immersing myself in the arts has kept me sane. Without it, I would have sunk into deep despair.

Making the immortelles is not all about death—far from it. The research and planning are enlightening. In doing so, I have learned much about the symbolism of birds and animals, plants and sea-creatures. I have discovered how different religions and cultures throughout history viewed such things, revered them or feared them, and together with what I learned from reading Mamgu's notes, my knowledge has increased substantially.

And then, of course, there is my studio work. I am inspired by the work of the Martin Brothers, who produce exquisite bird sculptures and vessels decorated with sea creatures. One day I would like to experiment with their method of salt-glazing, but my current kiln is not fit for purpose.

My favorite piece by the brothers is a stoneware vase entitled *pot with dragons*. On a pale copper background, demonic serpents and fierce dragons are skilfully illustrated, giving the piece the feel of the Orient. I am also enamoured with their bird sculptures, some of which caricature the political adversaries, Gladstone and Disraeli. The heads of their Wally Birds can be removed to reveal a space for storing pipe tobacco, and I cannot help thinking of Captain Thomas when I see them.

If Rowena were still here, I am sure she would have loved their work, too, and might have enjoyed replicating some of their strange pieces. Knowing her, she would have sculpted a Wally

Bird of her own, one which resembled Father Kendrick with a glowering expression and eyes black as obsidian. It would be in the form of a solitary magpie—one for sorrow—with its head and torso glazed satin black and a white collar like the reverend's. We would have laughed together, and I would have insisted she keep it in her bedroom in case he saw it. The magpie was the one bird Rowena disliked. When she was young, she would cover her ears at the sound of its throaty caw. "Why does it need to quarrel, Mam?" she would ask, and I knew what she meant.

Or am I fantasizing about such a scenario? Rowena made it clear before her accident that she did not intend to work in the pottery with me when she finished school. She did not want to become my apprentice, nor did she wish to remain in this little piece of paradise on the Welsh coast. I remember her words, though it pains me to do so. "When I leave school this summer, I want to go into service. I don't want to work in the pottery," she said, her mouth all pinched and the air between us frosty.

I would give anything to freeze time, to freeze her at that moment until she told me what caused her to behave so vehemently, for I still believe she kept something secret.

CHAPTER FOURTEEN

The resonant sound of a tolling bell jolts me awake, and for a moment I imagine I must be dreaming. I sit up and listen, sleepy eyes attempting to focus on the bedroom window through which the mother moon usually grants me light. But tonight, the sky is black as a demon—no moon, no stars, and I wonder where they have disappeared. My heart races. Never before has the church bell tolled in the middle of the night.

Silent now—silent as the grave. My breathing steadies, and I am about to lie back down when the sound comes again. Six resonant tolls, slow and ominous, followed by a minute's silence. This time, I am certain. It is the sound of the death knell.

I have no idea what time it is but assume it must be around two in the morning. I leap out of bed, wrap my shawl around my shoulders, and open the window. Brittle night air blasts my face, making me shiver. My bare feet protest against the cold floor-boards, but I stand stock-still and listen.

When it comes again, I know I must act. Perhaps there has

been another shipwreck, and maybe it is Father Kendrick's way of calling to the villagers for help. With unsteady hands I manage to light the lamp, then scramble for my clothes. Untamed hair and buttons fastened haphazardly are of little importance. Now is not the time to worry about one's appearance.

I am halfway down the lane, heading in the direction of the church, when the toll stops again. I freeze and listen, expecting any minute to see Bethan come dashing toward me as she did when the *Mary Anne* was wrecked in the storm. I expect, at least, to hear distant voices of alarm. Instead, I am greeted with an eerie silence. No howl from the wind, no scream from the fox, nothing but the sound of my own blood pounding in my ears.

I am torn between returning to the warmth and comfort of my bed or pressing on toward the church. I do not fear the dark—never have—and if I return home, I know I will not be able to go back to sleep because I am too alert, and full of adrenaline, with the curiosity of a cat.

I press on, guided by the rhythmic lap of the sea, her breath a sizzle as it caresses the shore and a gasp as she sucks a mouthful back. The slow rhythm steadies my breathing, and the distant beam from the lighthouse, which seems to flash in time with the waves, illuminates the scene in a sweeping arc.

Eventually I arrive at the church, expecting to be greeted by others. But there is no one. The church is not lit and the single bell, perched in its tower, glares down on me as though I am some kind of mischievous intruder.

I plant my feet on the ground, hands on hips, and glower back. *You were the one who woke me, so don't get all high and mighty.* I turn in a circle, unsure of what to do next. Never before have I been in the graveyard at night. Twilight, yes, but not when it's pitch dark. It is the most surreal experience, supernatural almost, like a scene from Wilkie Collins's *The Woman in White*. And I realize Rowena spends every night here and my heart plummets. I hope she is not afraid.

And then a strange notion enters my head: what if I am dead? What if the bell rang for me, and I am here as a ghost? The prospect of such a thing fails to alarm me; in fact, I am numb to the idea. I raise a hand in front of my face, and take deep breaths in and out, blowing onto my frigid palm. It warms, a sensation of damp condensation remains behind. I am not a ghost; therefore,

I need to find my logic and try to discover the reason for the tolling of the bell. Whoever rang it is likely to be inside the church, or else I would have passed them on my way here.

I grasp the sturdy metal door handle with my right hand, its piercing cold a painful warning, and enter. "Hello," I call, stepping into the pitch-black nave. Nothing. No voice, no footsteps, not even the scurry of a rogue mouse or a flutter of wings from a nesting bird. "Is anyone here?" My voice echoes back in the void, my sole companion. The absence of light envelops me, cocoons me in its blackness, and I shiver.

As I step back into the graveyard, the sweeping arc from the lighthouse briefly showcases the graves and my immortelles, spotlighting my work in a theatrical fashion. My eyes fall on Rowena's grave, the snowdrops inside her immortelle a pearlescent luster in the cold light of the arc. I stand transfixed, waiting for the sweeping arm of the beam to return. *Five, six, seven.* I am rewarded with a second glimpse, though it is soon snatched away as the beam sweeps across other graves.

And then I hear it, a bell ringing. Except this time it is not the mighty peal from the bell on the tower; this time it is a gentle *ding*. Rowena's bell, or bells I should say. Three tiny balls of silver, one at the centre of each snowdrop in place of a stigma, are calling me.

I find my feet, and scramble over grassy clumps and broken tombstones toward her grave. I watch, desperate for the sweeping arc of light to return so that my eyes can prove what my ears insist is happening.

I am not mistaken. Each beam reveals a slight shiver of ceramic petal, accompanied by a distinct *ding*, which would be lost to the wind if the night were not so still. She has called me at last. But why? Why now, in the middle of a winter's night?

My hand is placed flat against the glass dome, sensing the vibration of sound. It reminds me of when she was in the womb, how I would place my hand to my belly and feel her moving inside me. *What is it, Rowena?* I am in turmoil. Thrilled she has come to me after such a long wait, but desperate to understand what she wants.

It is a minute or so later that the sound stops. It is an odd feeling, a kind of tight-chested panic in case she does not return. The fact she was here at all is some consolation, progress of some kind, for she has never called me before.

I remain a while longer in case the ringing should start again and until my knees throb in protest at the cold ground. As I rise to my feet, the sweeping arc of light shines on the stone wall surrounding the graveyard. For a moment, I believe my eyes deceive me. I do not move a muscle, and am afraid to take a breath in case I frighten her off. I wait, and as the beam sweeps back around, my suspicion is confirmed. Crouched low in front of the wall in the corner of the graveyard is the figure of a young girl. *Rowena?*

The beam from the lighthouse taunts me as it plays hide-and-go-seek, and all I can do is wait until it decides to return. A matter of seconds feels like an age. I am sweating despite the icy temperature, and at the same time shivering. I clasp my teeth together to stop them from chattering, afraid that even the slightest sound might frighten her off. But as the beam returns, I know it is not Rowena. This girl is slighter, smaller in stature and fair-haired. And those eyes. Round as buttons, set in porcelain skin with hollowed shadows. Before I can take in any further detail, the beam moves on and I am once again plunged into darkness.

I call out to her in as soft a voice as I can manage, but she doesn't reply. And by the time the beam returns again, she is gone.

It is not until daylight hints at my bedroom window that I manage to fall asleep. When I wake it is past eight o'clock and memories of the previous night come flooding back. I dress and make my way into the kitchen where I proceed to riddle the range into life before adding more coal.

As I pour the tea there is a knock at the door. It is Gwyneth, and I cannot help but wish she were not such an early bird. I am undecided whether or not to tell her about my nighttime escapade. She already doubts my sanity, and I fear such a story might worry her.

But at a glance I see it is not my state of mind she has come to talk about. Her mournful expression suggests she bears worse news, and indeed she does. The body of a young girl has been discovered on the beach and is suspected to be that of Carys Morgan, the daughter of the former clerk of the works at Abereiddy stone quarry.

IMMORTELLE

Gwyneth tells me the girl had been missing since yesterday afternoon, and despite an extensive search the previous evening, which had for obvious reasons been called off after dusk, she was not found. Not until this morning when, according to Gwyneth, her broken body was discovered below the cliffs. It is believed she was swept in with the tide. Fully clothed, with a gash to her head, and limbs contorted into impossible angles, suggestive of a fall from the cliffs, she was pronounced dead at the scene.

The news floors me, but I am not surprised. Now I am desperate for Gwyneth to leave so that I might think things through. I offer little in the way of conversation, and Gwyneth assumes the news is too reminiscent of Rowena's death, so after a quick cup of tea she bids me farewell.

I cannot say I knew Carys well. I do, however, remember her glowering at church because her sullen expression reminded me of Rowena's. Gwyneth says she was as bright as a button, a bit of a tomboy by all accounts, often to be found barefoot on the beach or lost in some make-believe world amongst the gorse or churchyard.

I am reminded of the sickening shock when I was told Rowena's body had been found and cannot help but dwell on how Carys's mother must be feeling. No doubt I shall know more soon, and perhaps be called upon by Mrs. Morgan if an immortelle is to be made in memory of her daughter.

But what is evident, at least to me, is that the previous night Rowena called out to me to warn me of Carys's accident. Did Rowena's ghost witness her fall, or was the ringing of the bells Rowena's attempt at raising the alarm when the girl's body washed in on the tide? One thing I am certain of: it was Carys's ghost which presented itself at the graveyard last night.

CHAPTER FIFTEEN

Two weeks have passed since the news of Carys's death. I said nothing to Gwyneth about my middle of the night jaunt, nor did I mention the tolling of the bell. As I imagined, Carys's mother visited the day after the funeral to ask me to make an immortelle for her daughter's grave. Of course I agreed, though I have to say her demeanour was a little cold and distant.

Before meeting her, I assumed our conversation would be easy, especially as we share such a life-changing experience, but it was not. If I am honest, I found her somewhat stand-offish, her words regarding Carys seemed distant and unemotional. She seemed the fussy type, the kind of person who is inclined to find fault. She requested the immortelle be bright and cheerful, something befitting a young girl with a tendency to stray from the straight and narrow, and I found it an odd description given the circumstances, especially as it was said with no hint of warmth. Perhaps the shock has not yet manifested itself.

Carys's immortelle will be a riot of color and sunshine in

memory of the girl who ran with the wind.

I am rolling clay in preparation for the daisies when I sense her presence. The air chills, mists, and for a few moments I cannot see a hand in front of my face. She stands behind me, I'm sure. Whoever is there, and I am inclined to think it is Carys, has brought the smell of the grave with them, though it is not unpleasant. It is an earthy scent, like the woods after a downpour of rain.

My instinct is to turn around, but I resist. I have learned from previous encounters that the dead are as sensitive as the living to sudden movement, and I do not wish to frighten her off.

The mist clears as she sidles closer, appearing on my left, a shadow of her former self but nonetheless recognizable. It is Carys, as I suspected. Has she come out of curiosity, or is there another reason? I am reminded of how similar she was in personality to Rowena, though not in appearance. In appearance they were chalk and cheese. Rowena was fair-skinned, tall, with chestnut hair that tumbled to her waist in bountiful ringlets that refused to be tamed. Carys, on the other hand, is petite in stature, with cornflower eyes and hair the color and texture of straw. I steal a glimpse out of the corner of my eye as I reach for the fettling knife. She is pale, translucent almost. She leans an elbow on the worktop and in a confident voice, caught somewhere between childhood and womanhood, she speaks.

"I've come to see you," she says, and waits to see if I will react. I have learned to allow the dead to speak their minds without interrupting. Her sigh, when it comes, is the breathless kind. "Your tributes to the dead leave me spellbound and have always done so." Still I say nothing, though a fist of emotion squeezes my throat. "You should take it as a compliment, you know. Like Mother, I am not easily impressed. I imagine you think my interest in grave ornaments is rather macabre for one so young." She seems eager to affirm her tenacious nature, though having met her mother, I am not surprised. "I know your immortelles so well that should some diafol remove them from the graves and discard them in the field, I could return them to their rightful owners without hesitation."

She seems proud of the fact, and I purse my lips to prevent a smile.

"Oak leaves—the symbol of hospitality—for Alys Pritchard, former landlady of The Ferry Inn. A sheaf of wheat and a wee scythe for Hywel Jones of Gwbert Farm, and the one I favor most—the bay leaf and bluebell—symbols of fame and sorrowful regret for Mari Howell, for she sang like the angels." Her ghostly form pirouettes, scrawny arms outstretched as she raises her eyes to the ceiling.

It seems she recognizes my work almost as well as I do, but I sense she has not come to talk about the immortelles, not really. She steadies herself, drags soil-encrusted fingers through matted hair, and runs a purpling tongue around lips cracked and dry as autumn leaves.

She whispers, close to my ear, and for the first time I am a little afraid. "I must tell someone what happened to me." Again she waits, but I will not look in her direction, nor will I allow my breath to give me away. If I engage her in conversation, I will become emotional. I prefer to hear what she has to say before interacting with the supernatural.

"I choose to confide in you because I have seen the way you watch Father Kendrick through narrowed eyes, the way you avoid his handshake as we traipse from Sunday Matins with our souls washed clean. I think you do so because you do not believe in his childish God, and because like me, you recognize in him something of the underworld. We attend his services because we must—because it is what everyone here does without question, but we do not have to like the man, do we?"

At the mention of his name, I cannot help but gasp, but she does not seem to notice.

"What I have to say will be of great interest to you," she says, with all the confidence of a bird taking to the air. "But before I begin, I shall allow you to gather your needs, for Mother has high standards and will not tolerate second best. I know she wants yellow for my immortelle, yellow and white, with perhaps a touch of greenery. I remember her words when you met with her last week. When she came, her eyes were swollen with counterfeit tears, which did not surprise me." She lowers her head, pulls at the front of her once-white shroud. "I see everything you know, though the living only see me if I want them to. Focus now, or you shall attract the wrath of Mother's tongue, as did I on many occasions."

In one swift movement she hoists herself onto the slab of the worktop and sits knees to chest, making herself small so as to provide me enough space to work. And her breath is silent. Non-existent. It does not condense on the frozen windowpane, even though her forehead is pressed hard to it. She has no reflection either. I suppose she shall get used to such things.

For several minutes she amuses herself with the view out the window whilst I gather the materials, humming a tune as I do so. She will no doubt recognize it, *Suo Gân,* a Welsh lullaby...

Ni chaiff dim amharu'th gyntun
Ni wna undyn â thi gam...

Nothing shall disturb your slumber
Nobody will do you harm...

My worktop is prepared: bone china clay, pale as the death mask; sharply pointed sticks for veining leaves through which blood no longer flows; and lastly a vessel of water, though I doubt it's anointed. It shall suffice.

She senses I am ready to listen and begins...

"The first time a man of God held me above the water I raged a storm, my lungs a fit of temper. Fists balled and complexion red as your madder root... or so Mother tells me, for I was barely a month old, and have no memory of my baptism. With his thumb, Father Michael marked the sign of the cross on my wrinkled forehead before passing me to Aunt Eira, my godmother, named for the snow.

The second time was different, but I shall come to that."

I roll the clay and begin to shape daisies, the symbol of innocence. My fingers work deftly, moulding and shaping the clay before joining each tiny petal to the carpels—the female reproductive organs. And all the while my breathing is regular, steady. I give nothing away.

"By the age of seven, Mother decided I was old enough to play outdoors unaccompanied. My father had not long passed, and I believe she found my constant presence an irritation. 'Stay well away from the sea and don't go climbing the cliffs,' she'd say, confident I would do her bidding.

"During summer I wandered the fields above the beach,

gathering witches' thimbles and hare's foot clover, though according to lore neither should be picked for fear of bringing about disaster. I would tumble my way down to the beach and paddle barefoot in the cold Irish Sea, the arm of the North Atlantic, and gaze toward the horizon dreaming of another life, in another land. Did you know the next stop is America, and that many hereabouts have sailed to a place called Pennsylvania in the hope of a better future?" She pauses momentarily. "But my favorite playground of all was the churchyard on the clifftop—the place of song and psalm, lies and truths, blessings and burials."

I bend and shape the daisy stems, as she watches. She is eager to see what I will create next. I pause, my clay-choked fingers poised at the edge of the worktop, contemplating. A moment's indecision. Because she watches, I feel a tremendous sense of responsibility, though I imagine if something displeases her she will not hesitate to tell me. All I have to go on are my own memories and the words of Carys's mother to help me choose.

There is an air of tension as I waver, undecided, and reach for my sketchbook. She sidles closer, and peers over my shoulder, her long sun-bleached hair tickling my neck. I hold my breath, surprised by the invasion of personal space. Then, she plants the lightest of kisses above my ear, and it is hard not to flinch.

With a lopsided grin she shuffles back to her space on the worktop, her ghostly frame making no sound in doing so. I need to regain my nerve, so I flip through page after page of sketches. I dismiss most and pause briefly at others until finally, I stop dead at a sprig of orange blossom. I tilt my head and draw air deep into my lungs, imagining its heady scent. The decision is made; my next floral tribute will be orange blossom—the symbol of chastity.

The daisy petals were child's play compared to this task, though my fingers do not tremble as I cut and form each tiny petal, for I am well-practiced.

She watches with bated breath in case their delicate form should break, though why she finds it necessary to do so, I cannot say. She has no breath. It is simply a habit. A nod of approval, then she takes up her story where she left off.

"I suppose you remember Father Michael, the man who christened me? I liked him, but I never took to his replacement, Father Kendrick. On occasion, he would observe me at play, stern black cassock and starched white collar in opposition to his outward amiable demeanour. If I saw him first, I would run and hide amongst the gravestones, playing peek-a-boo. I believe he considered me a little wild, at least at play, for Mother made sure I was on my best behavior during his sermons."

I am reminded of Rowena and hide a smile.

"He was supposed to be the pillar of our community, respected by all, even though it is whispered he is partial to more than a sip of communion wine, but I never felt at ease in his company. It was his eyes, you see. Those dark orbs, impassive as the lens of a daguerreotype camera."

She shudders and fades in and out like the moon behind clouds.

"I believe I had reached the age of eleven before he approached me. I knelt at your daughter's grave... may I say, her immortelle is a remarkable piece! Though, I find your choices rather peculiar: snowdrops—the symbol of hope—bow their heads in respect, but a starling of all things! Its speckled feathers in shades of iridescent purple and green and beaded with tiny cream seed pearls. Why did you include that particular bird? It seems an odd thing for a child. Mother says it's because the starling carries a message from the spirit world, but I'd like to be certain.

Your mother is right, Carys, but I also chose the starling for its color.

"Forgive me, I digress. Father Kendrick caught me deep in thought and startled me. 'What is it about those that fascinates you so?' he asked, causing me to lose my balance and almost topple onto the glass dome. What a disaster that would have been!" She giggles, and it echoes around the room. "I had the impression he was not overly enamored with your work; perhaps he considered it frivolous. I did not quite know how to answer him, so I shrugged and shook my head.

"'The dead interest you—a morbid fascination for one so young,' he said, glowering beneath heavy brows. He crouched beside me, his thigh grazing mine, and I smelled his sour breath and something else—a sickly sweet note that I could not identify. I was sure he noticed my look of distaste as I sprang to my feet and stepped away.

"It is not death which fascinates me," I said, "but art."

"'Then next time you come I shall show you our stained glass window. And there are other works besides within,' he said, nodding in the direction of the church.

"I gave no response. Of course I knew the window of which he spoke—it is of The Virgin Mary, without child. I imagine you know of it, too. I did not desire a private sermon from him, albeit one on art. You see, when my father died, I lost my faith, though of course I hid it from Mother. She'd have whacked me into submission if she'd known, though it would have changed nothing, for faith is absolute—once it escapes, it rarely returns."

I find myself nodding in agreement and hope she doesn't notice.

"I avoided the churchyard afterwards. Instead, I watched from the beach and began to learn the exact time of his coming and going. That way, I could indulge my interest without risking his presence."

I have finished forming the orange blossom. My neck aches both from tension and from the hours spent leaning over the worktop. I stretch and yawn. The light has dimmed. The sun is setting. I stand and place the tray of flowers to dry. Carys seems to sense the hour, too.

"I'll bid you goodnight," she says, "or else I might stay beyond my allotted time. Go to your bed now, as I shall to mine, though yours is warm and dry whilst mine is not. Tomorrow I shall return."

All night, Carys's words haunt me far more than her ghost. The thought of her returning to a cold, damp bed sickens me. My stomach churns at the thought of Rowena lying in her grave conscious of such discomfort. The illogical part of me wants to remove Rowena's body from the ground and bring her home where it is warm and dry. At the same time, I realize how ludicrous the thought is.

And what did Carys mean when she spoke of allotted time? I think back to the ghost of the sailor on the beach and to Captain Thomas. One seen at night, and the other by day.

I fret over her words for some considerable time. What does it matter how long a ghost wanders? Who is there to insist they return to the grave? And what punishment might await their disobedience? It is all too complex. Too upsetting to think about. I prefer to believe she referred to her time on earth when her mother would call her home before dark. In all likelihood, Carys still imagines this to be the case. Her ghost lives by earthly rules of childhood memories.

And the talk of Father Kendrick seems to suggest he had a part to play in her death. If that is the case, then it seems my instinct was right all along.

The following morning, and despite the lack of sleep, I take up my work with renewed vigour. Fuelled by adrenaline, I cannot wait to hear the next installment. I long for her return. I need to know how the story ends and sense that soon I will have answers as to what happened to Rowena. I never would have imagined the answers to arrive via a ghost.

I do not have long to wait. No sooner have I gathered my materials than I sense her presence. She sits on the worktop, just as she did yesterday.

I roll the clay and begin by shaping a primrose.

"What color will it be?" she asks, and I almost answer. I clear my throat to prevent her noticing. "Yellow, I hope," she says, "for then my place of rest will shine out above all others. I can't wait until you glaze. Why, the sheer alchemy of the process! How does the heat from the flames cause such changes?" She raises a hand in front of my face, and turns her head to the side. "No—do not explain, or it will delay my story further." She flicks a woodlouse from her lap and rubs at a stain on her shroud to no effect.

I am eager to hear what happened next, desperate to know of Father Kendrick's involvement.

"I could have set my clock by his time-keeping," she says, "and so I was surprised to hear Father Kendrick's voice. I had spent the morning at the beach searching for bivalves and ammonites to add to my collection and needed to rest. Certain of at least an hour before he would return, I entered the church, leaving the door ajar, and stood examining the stained glass. I do not know how he managed to approach without me hearing.

"'So you have come at last,' he said, 'I assumed you'd lost interest.'"

"It had been several weeks since that day at the grave, the day he first spoke to me about art, so I would not have imagined him to remember. I cannot say exactly why his presence made me uncomfortable; call it a sixth sense. A twitching smirk played at the corners of his mouth. I thought it best to be polite, in case he tittle-tattled to mother.

"Good afternoon, Father, I said, my attention focused on the stained glass window.

"He drew closer until the heat of his body warmed my bare arms. I'd not thought to carry my shawl, not with the sun so fierce, though Mother would have disapproved. Instead, I wrapped my arms about myself, protectively.

"The mother of Jesus watched in her sanctimonious fashion, the brilliant sunshine outside causing her to appear especially ethereal. 'The Virgin Mary,' he said, as though he considered me ignorant of the fact. Stale breath, smelling faintly of wine, tickled my ear, and another scent too—like the blooms of the hawthorn—the smell of decay.

"I stepped closer to the window in an attempt to put some distance between us. 'I must go now, Father,' I said, desperate to make my escape. I turned to leave but found my way barred by him and the pews. My heart fluttered, and a trickle of cold sweat ran down my spine. 'Excuse me Father,' I said, but still he did not move."

I have turned my attention to the stigma. With tips of fingers and thumbs, I roll the tiniest piece of clay into a funnel shape. Her body (if that is what it can be called, for really it is no more than a shadow) rocks gently to and fro, in time to my movement, and the tip of her tongue projects from between her teeth. I am filled with a sudden sense of outrage. Like Rowena, she was just a child. But I must remain calm and listen.

"'Come into the vestry,' he said. 'Within there are works of art the likes of which you cannot imagine.'

"Words failed me; I could think of no plausible excuse for refusing him. Meek as the lamb, I trailed behind. He gestured for me to sit in front of a desk. Behind him stood a case of ancient tomes, so thick with dust I could have written my name to evidence my being there. But it was not one of those he chose but another, hidden behind lock and key.

"'You are not the first to lose faith,' he said, his expression stern, 'nor will you be the last.' He turned the tome to face me.

"'But, Father, I—' Raising a finger he silenced me, and the charnel pits which were his eyes held me captive. He tapped the book, as would a schoolmaster, a gesture I took to mean I should open it. My fingers trembled and my palms grew damp, but I dared not defy him.

"How to describe the images within? Bloody, grotesque, yet at the same time beautiful. Each page protected by an opaque film, I could but anticipate the image concealed beneath. Engrossed in its contents, I forgot his presence.

"Each print depicted a satanic scene—a tableau of the diabolical—and though the subjects were abhorrent, I was bewitched. The names of the artists were printed at the bottom of each page. Some I recognized: Blake's *Great Red Dragon and the Beast from the Sea*, Fuseli's *Nightmare*, with an incubus sat upon a sleeping woman's abdomen. But others I could never have imagined—scenes of hell and devils, the dead and decaying—certainly a tome unsuited to a priest's possession.

"I grew aware of my breathing, deep and slow, a shudder at the turn of each page. And then something distracted me—a lazy buzzing sound. I raised my head, attempting to locate its source. A bluebottle fly landed in front of him, silent now as it rubbed its legs together. Quick as a wink, he snatched it up and closed his fist. I gasped, for I have always found it an impossible task.

"He watched me closely, amused by my surprise. 'The images meet your approval, I see,' he said, a smirk upon his flaky, gray lips. And he was right, though his recognition of such caused me to feel tainted. 'I have something else to show you,' he said, reaching with one hand to open a drawer. From the other hand came the frenzied, muted buzz of the fly. He took out a dagger, its metal so polished it dazzled my eyes. Engraved upon its hilt was an inverted pentagram. Before I had time to think, he opened his fist and released the fly, which appeared to kneel before him on the desk, as though in praise. Swift as a hare, he cleaved it in two down the middle—one now-blind compound eye watched me, the other him."

I have constructed the leaves and am marking the veins. My fingers slip and I make an imprecise cut. In temper I scrunch the leaf into a ball and toss it into the clay bin. Carys pauses, and for a moment I believe I have betrayed myself and that she knows I hear. But I have not. She needed a moment to prepare herself to explain what happened next.

"My heart beat like a drum—I felt sure he must hear it. He

placed the dagger on the desk, a smear of yellowish liquid upon the blade already congealing. Terrified, I stood. 'I must go, Mother will worry,' I said. Concerned he might attempt to bar my way, I hurried from the vestry, praying all the way down the aisle that he had not locked the main door behind him when he entered earlier. My legs trembled so badly I thought they might give way.

"All the way home I pondered over whether or not to confide in Mother. I doubted she would believe me. She was not enamored of me of late—not since discovering my choice of reading matter. 'It's written in the diafol's own hand,' she'd scolded. Sometimes I think the woman is a half-wit. I wonder... have you read the stories of Arthur Machen? I'm sure you would enjoy them. Mother studies only the Bible, well that and the *Cardigan Observer*."

I ignore her question and continue veining the leaf.

"By the time I reached home, I had calmed somewhat, and so decided to keep it from her, though I vowed never again to darken the door of the church unaccompanied. I would have loved to give up attendance altogether, but I believe Mother would have sent me to reform school at the mere suggestion. Of course, I should stay away from the graveyard, too, but how would I bear it?"

Today has been miserable and wet, and we have lost the light early, and besides, I have completed my task. The tray of flowers and leaves is full. I rise from the bench, eyelids drooping with exhaustion and my footsteps are laboured. The creation of Carys's immortelle and the horror of her story weighs heavy. A match has been struck to my grief.

I am overwhelmed with the certainty that Carys's story is coming to a climax, and at the same time both eager and in dread of hearing it. I would like her to see the immortelle complete, but that is not the real reason I stop work. I stop as a bribe, a way of ensuring her return tomorrow, and besides, I do not think I can take any more tonight, not without acknowledging her presence.

The following morning, at the stroke of nine, Carys appears at my side. Today she seems agitated. I am dismayed to find her hair sodden and clinging to her shoulders. Her fingernails are black, thick with earth, and her shroud is slick with mud. It rained during the night, and I cannot help but think this is the cause. I turn my back to her, place a hand over my mouth to stop myself from crying out. Is this how Rowena suffers? My head spins and I feel light-headed. I take deep breaths and try to calm myself. Carys wraps her arms about herself, rubs her shoulders, though her teeth do not chatter, nor does she shiver. Surely she cannot feel the cold? I want to comfort her and provide her with a warm blanket and a hot drink. Yet at the same time, I understand how ridiculous the thought is. It is a mother's instinct, though. No—it is the instinct of any decent human being to care for a child. Her voice, when it comes, seems a little fainter and has a rasping quality.

"What a temper the heavens displayed last night!" she says, and the sockets of her eyes are dark shadows set in alabaster skin. "The pounding of the rain above my head and the roaring thunder disturbed me from my sleep. Did it wake you? I believe it must have, for the skin beneath your eyes resembles that of the thundercloud."

Her forthright manner amuses me, and some of my sorrow ebbs away. She takes up her usual position at the corner of my worktop and watches in fascination as I weave my magic. Perched high on a shelf above my head is a row of neatly labeled glass jars, each filled to varying degrees with white powder. I don a pair of surgical gloves and a mask, and make my selection: phosphorus, silicate... arsenic.

"Arsenic?" she says. "Am I correct in thinking arsenic is a poison? Thank goodness you are protected. Of course, it does not matter that I am not." She suppresses a giggle by putting a hand to her mouth. "Why, I could consume the whole jar and it would do me no further harm. Which reminds me—have you read Machen's *Novel of the White Powder*? It really is quite gruesome. The protagonist's sick brother is prescribed a white powder, which changes him into a writhing, putrid mass. Small wonder Mother was aghast when she found it, I suppose, but then I didn't ask her to read it."

Her expression changes from one of wicked joy to one of fear. Cornflower eyes dim and turn hazy.

"It was Father Kendrick who loaned me the book, you know, and I'm afraid what I have to tell you today may cause you upset."

My brushes are laid out before me in readiness for glazing. This part of the process requires a steady hand. I hope I can manage it. She watches closely as my wrist bends and contracts with each stroke of the brush, lower lip bitten in concentration.

Her chest cavity expands and contracts as she prepares to tell the next installment, though her lungs do not fill with air. It is the strangest sight.

"Where was I?" She places a gnarled finger to her lip, and raises an eyebrow. "Ah, yes," she says, "The incident with the fly and the dagger... Afterwards, apart from the obligatory Sunday Matins, I managed to avoid him. Intending to make the most of summer's last blessings, I had spent all day at the beach. After lunch, which consisted of a hunk of bread torn from Mother's warm loaf and some sharp cheese, I decided to explore the rocks further up the cliff. The tide had reached its highest, and so many of the rock pools I'd scavenged amongst earlier were now submerged.

"Removing my boots and placing them out of harm's reach (for I knew what a scolding I would receive from Mother should they be swept away), I scrambled up the rocks. I was adept at climbing—a mountain goat of sorts. Crouched before a promising rock pool, the last of the sun's rays warming my back, a sudden chill made me look up.

"There he stood, his white shirt slick with sweat and his hair plastered to his head like some demon birthed from the sea. I gasped in shock, edged away, putting faith in my bare feet to find their hold on the seaweed-slick rocks.

"He made no attempt at small talk. Instead his right hand slipped around his back and removed the dagger. Evil as sin, he came toward me. Turning away, I ran, and cried out with pain as the soft flesh of my soles was torn by the limpets' shells.

"But he was too quick. Swift and sure-footed, he pursued me toward the cliff's edge. All too soon, it fell away toward the ravenous sea. I swayed on my feet, bare arms half-raised at my sides, ready to take flight."

My breathing quickens and my brush is poised in mid-air. On my forehead beads of perspiration threaten to run. The temperature does not cause it, but tension. I wipe away the sweat in the sleeve of my shirt.

"The blade or the sea? No time to waver. Should I choose the blade, he would know victory, and my soul would be his. He sensed my hesitation and grabbed for my arm. Swift and lithe, I yanked it from his grasp. I chose the sea and plummeted gracelessly toward its waiting bosom. For a split second, it seemed I might make it, but I had forgotten that the rocks, which an hour earlier had yielded their gifts, now lay submerged."

She pauses, and gathers herself before delivering the final blow.

"The snap of my neck was the last thing I heard."

My hands are frozen. In the first two fingers and thumb of my left hand, I hold the frail stem of a daisy, and with my right, I snap. The broken stem—symbolic of the moment of death. Her voice shudders, a sobbing quality but without the usual inclusion of air. It is the strangest sound and it is all I can do to stop myself from comforting her. She takes a few moments to calm herself, then continues.

"Recall, if you will, my words when I spoke of my baptism; I said the second time a man of God held me above the water was different. Now I shall explain.

"He stood knee deep, and the seething tide offered up my broken body into his waiting arms. He held me aloft and wailed toward the heavens. It really was quite grotesque—the way in which my head hung limp and contorted at an impossible angle, though now I find the memory almost humorous.

"And I was calm; all fear was swallowed by the waves. I sat cross-legged on the sand, watching, though when I stood I left no indent. It was over; that was all that mattered. I was free, and he was defeated; a lifeless offering cannot be offered up for sacrifice. I am certain that had been his intention.

"He carried my body to the cave, and hid it deep inside, before returning just before dawn at the turning of the tide so that he might pretend the sea had brought me home."

She uncrosses her legs, folds them beneath her, and places her hands in her lap.

"And there you have it. My story is told," she says. "Tomorrow I shall return one last time, for I wish to see the immortelle complete."

I dare not look at her, or she will read the despair on my face. I am certain now—certain Rowena, too, suffered at his hands. She follows me outdoors, watches as I place the tray into the kiln.

I stoop to light it, my eyes following the dance of the flames as they spring to life. The air has chilled. I rub my shoulders and blow on my fingers to warm them before making my way indoors.

I infuse a pot of peppermint tea. It is all I can stomach. Tonight the sky is clear and the constellation Aquarius is framed at the window. I throw a log on the fire, and watch it spit and cackle a tiding of encouragement. But the night sky demands my attention. Aquarius pours his nectar from an amphora straight into the mouth of the fish... and I know what it is I must do.

The morning dawns still and cold. Overnight, the sea has delivered a blanket of gray mist, one which is determined to stay and watch over proceedings. On the worktop, Carys's floral offerings are arranged with precision on a bed of dried moss. It is exquisite, even if I say so myself. All that remains is to place the glass dome on top of the display and seal it for eternity.

Carys sits in her usual spot. She seems on edge, fidgeting with the graying cuffs of her shroud and pulling loose threads so that the fabric frays. She fades in and out like the memories of the elderly. I assume that having offloaded she has not been granted the satisfaction she imagined. She will, though, for I have a trick or two up my sleeve. She frowns, folds her arms across her chest, and waits. This girl is inquisitive, just like Rowena. I fuss over a tray of cups and a plate of cake and her mood brightens.

"Ah," she says, and her ghostly face lights up. "You must be expecting a visitor. Of course, it will be Mother. No doubt she wants to view my memorial before it is sealed in case she desires something to be altered. Do not be surprised if she complains a little. Mother is not easily pleased and is capable of picking fault with perfection."

Her expression changes again to one of uncertainty. She does not seem keen on seeing her mother. It is then she notices the carafe of red wine and an empty glass.

"You are mistaken," she says. "Mother does not partake of the diafol's brew. You will need to put the kettle on if you are to appeal to her taste."

I lift the carafe by its neck and hold it to the window, swirling its contents round and round. My reflection is flushed and distorted in the convex glass of the carafe. Something in the garden catches my attention. A murder of crows has gathered in the ash tree, their throaty caws alerting me to my visitor's arrival. The door opens, but it is not Carys's mother who stands on the threshold. I was not expecting it to be. "Good afternoon, Father," I say, a hand outstretched in welcome.

Out of the corner of my eye I sense Carys has frozen. She steeples her fingers and holds them to her lips. She is trembling, and the air chills a degree or two. Why had I not considered her fear? How selfish of me to assume that because she is beyond physical harm his presence would not frighten her. I am confident he does not see her, but of course she sees him. And worse than that, she will think me a traitor. Having put her faith in me she will imagine I have let her down. The urge to allay her fears is overwhelming, but of course I cannot—not yet.

"Is it ready?" he asks, and I nod toward Carys's immortelle which lies in wait on the slab.

"So it is to receive its post-mortem from the devil then," she whispers in my ear.

"A little wine, Father?" I say, lifting the carafe to his nose.

Momentarily he hesitates, then nods.

I pour, but not without first swirling the carafe again. My hand trembles, and I spill a little. Both Carys and I watch him, his attention fixed on the flowers. He *mmm's* and *ahhh's*, feigning interest, and it is then she notices the open jars atop the bench: cobalt, lead, lithium, arsenic, and in an instant she understands what it is I have done.

I hand him the glass, and he gulps greedily. Within seconds, it is drained. "You must be thirsty, Father," I say, doing my best to curtail the tremble in my voice. "Would you like another?"

As I pour, his pallor pales. A sweat breaks out upon his face and his lips turn blue. Clutching his throat, he yowls like the devil and Carys presses her hands to her ears. As he falls, I step back, my face as intense as the flames from the kiln. He utters a choking gurgle as a bubbling spurt of blackened liquid foams from his mouth. Then, he is still.

Carys is frozen to the spot. She stares down at the body, wide-eyed and trembling.

I face her then for the first time and hold out my hands, though I know I cannot touch her. "It is over, Carys," I say. "Go to your rest now, sweet girl, and leave this to me. He cannot hurt you, nor can he do the same to another child."

Our eyes lock, and we nod at one another. My throat constricts with dregs of sentiment. There is nothing more that needs to be said.

She is gone, and I am alone. What I must do next defies all logic and reviles me to the core, but he must not be given the opportunity of a Christian burial.

In the shed behind the pottery is an axe and a saw, both razor sharp. I remove my apron and pull on full-length overalls and gloves, then I start by removing his legs.

I stoke the fire at the foot of the kiln and add more wood for good measure. The furnace is ravenous; excited flames dance and lick the air. The taste of death is on its tongue and it cannot wait to consume every morsel.

Every last scrap of flesh and bone has been fed to the furnace. Tomorrow, once the kiln has cooled, I shall perform my final act of alchemy.

CHAPTER SIXTEEN

I rise with the birds, though I barely slept a wink. A sense of morbid excitement courses through my veins, and I am breathless with anticipation. I step into the dawn. The sky is painted in muted stripes of lavender blue and blush pink, and the shadowed greenery is dark and sharp in contrast. Rowena's starling waits for me on the gatepost. She wears her winter coat, and her bill has darkened with the season. Her song is urgent, and she flaps her wings in a flamboyant fashion. I shoo her away because I do not want her to witness what I am about to do.

The temperature of the kiln had cooled during the night and for that I am grateful. The frosty air is still and silent as the grave. It seems to hold its breath as I open the door and peer into the firebox. Bones. Brittle bones which cinder at my touch and the taste of ash lingers on my tongue. I wrap my scarf around my nose and mouth, tie it tight at the back of my neck, before sweeping the remains into the bucket.

I am surprised at how calm I feel. No shame and no

remorse—just relief.

A scoop at a time, I add ashes and bone to the mortar before grinding them with a pestle, all the while chanting Mamgu's spell under my breath. My fingers inscribe invisible symbols in the air. Twice the amount of bone ash to clay is necessary for a hard-wearing, intense white china—white as the reverend's collar and far more pure than his heart.

Throughout the night I tossed and turned against a tide of emotion, deciding on what his immortelle should include, and came to this conclusion: deadly nightshade, its black berries attached to pentagram-shaped leaves, the symbol of deception, danger, and death, though harmless to birds. I shall add prickly thistles, epitomizing pain and pride, and of course a hard-shelled black and tan sexton beetle, the undertaker of the insect world which buries corpses to feast upon later. Like the reverend, it is willing to defer gratification.

Three days labour it will take to complete, the same length of time it took Jesus to rise from the dead. I have no intention of allowing such a thing to happen to Father Kendrick's soul. Instead, his will be encapsulated into the garden of evil and permanently sealed in a miniature glass coffin, which shall remain hidden in a locked cupboard in the pottery, perched between jars of lead and arsenic. No one will be any the wiser. I am now certain that just like Snow White, he used a poisonous apple to foil Rowena.

As I place his immortelle on the cupboard shelf, the door to the pottery opens with a bang, allowing a rush of brittle air to enter with it. Gwyneth stands there, hands on generous hips and breathless.

"I don't suppose you've seen Father Kendrick?" she says, untying a headscarf and plonking herself down on a stool that I cannot promise will hold her weight.

I swallow hard and hope my face does not give me away. "No, why?"

"He's not been seen since last Tuesday at Carys's funeral. He's not at home. I've checked."

"How strange," I say, turning my attention to a basin of hot, soapy water and a cloth. "No doubt he'll turn up." I wipe down the work surface with vigour. "Perhaps he's gone away for a few days."

"Ah, well," she says. "Just thought I'd check." She gives me her best gap-toothed grin. "I could murder a cuppa if you have time to indulge an old lady. And you could do with a slice of that cake I brought you the other day. You've gone all thin and scrawny again."

We sit and chat about this and that, and it is all I can do to stop myself shaking. I am not sorry for what I have done. I feel no sense of remorse or guilt, but Gwyneth is my closest friend, and this is the one thing I cannot confide. I suppose I shall have to get used to it. There is no other choice. Whatever the outcome, this is one secret I will take to my grave.

As she takes her leave, she says, "I suppose we'll have to give him a day or two then call the police."

My heart plummets, but I act the fool. "Police?"

"Father Kendrick. If he doesn't show up, someone'll have to look for him."

I laugh. "Sorry, Gwyn. I'd completely forgotten. Let me know if there's any news."

I close the door, lean my back against it, and gather my breath. I must get a grip of my emotions or I am at risk of giving myself away. Why had I not considered the repercussions?

Another three days pass by before Gwyneth once again comes calling. I am clearing out the tool shed and the axe and saw lie on the floor in a heap, disguising themselves amongst more innocent tools. Their handles and teeth have been scrubbed clean of sin, and their souls shine bright as new. No one would suspect them of taking part in a crime.

Her cheeks are ruddy, her brow furrowed, and I know in an instant what she has come to say. "I have news, but you will need to sit down to hear it."

My heart leaps to my throat. Why does she insist I sit? Do her words imply my involvement? "Is it about Father Kendrick?" I say. I have no need of a mirror to tell me how pale I am or how my pupils are dilated to the size of pennies.

"Indeed," she says.

I wipe the dirt from my hands on an old cloth and lead the way indoors. My legs threaten to give way as I walk, and my mouth is parched. Once indoors, I busy myself with the kettle so that I do not have to look at her.

"Sit down, bach, you need to hear this."

I do as she bids me. She seems agitated. A myriad of thoughts whirl through my mind. She knows I am guilty. But then why Gwyneth and not the police? Surely the police would come if I am under suspicion.

"Now then," she says, taking my hand in hers. "I don't quite know how to say this, but it seems you were not wrong when you imagined Father Kendrick might be involved in Rowena's death." She takes a deep breath and her pale, old eyes fill with tears. "I'm sorry, Elinor."

Three hours and copious cups of tea later, she finally leaves. I am still in shock. It will take some time for me to digest all she told me. A secret cellar brimming with books and artefacts associated with devil worship and sacrifice. Strange objects preserved in jars of formaldehyde. All of this whispered in confidence, of course, since she has been sworn to secrecy by Constable Matthews.

A pillar of the community is Gwyneth. Not much escapes her ears. Quite how she managed to muscle her way in when the police searched his home I do not know. Perhaps it was her who raised the alarm in the first place. She might even have told me, I cannot remember. But I do know they took away a diary and notebook as well as a jar which contained a suspicious looking substance, a white powder of some kind, for analysis. I am certain it will reveal the poison that contributed to Rowena's death, though of course it is far too late to prove. For now, they assume he has either caused himself harm or fled without so much as a by your leave. I do not know how they can imagine the latter considering he left behind enough evidence to condemn him. "Unless they recover a body," she said, and my heart leapt. "Then they might think differently."

My mind is as turbulent as a storm. It cannot decide in which direction to gust, nor which towns to destroy. A sense of overwhelming grief has once again reared its ugly head and threatens to consume me, but it is more than that. I am furious because his part in Rowena's death will never be proven, and yet I know deep down I have wreaked revenge in the most satisfying way possible.

I am crippled because his part in Carys's death will not be so much as suspected, not unless the police find incriminating evidence in his diary or notebook. On the surface her death seems like an accident. I dare not admit that Carys came to me as a ghost and told me the truth, or they will whip me away to an institution and declare me insane.

Only time will tell. I shall have to be patient and wait for the outcome. I return to the tool shed and busy myself tidying its contents for the remains of the day.

Before I finish for the night, I must take a final look at his immortelle. The whole scenario is surreal, and I need to check it is not a figment of my imagination. I reach up and take it down from the cupboard shelf. Nothing inside it stirs, the beetle does not scurry among the flora, nor does it attempt to fly into the light from my lantern.

Satisfied nothing has moved or changed beneath the glass, I lift it back onto the shelf where it nestles comfortably between poisonous chemicals.

"Mam?" My back is to the door, and for a moment I am afraid to turn around.

"Rowena?"

She stands in the doorway, unsure whether or not to enter. My hands fly to my mouth and I moan. "Rowena!"

She steps forward, a silver-shadowed slip of a girl, and gazes into my eyes. Hers are deep pools of sorrow, her lower lip quivers with pent-up emotion.

My legs go from under me and I slump to the floor.

"It's all right, Mam," she says. "I'm all right... You made it so."

I reach out to her, longing to hold her tight, though I know it is not possible. She slips through my fingers like the sands of time and then she is gone.

I do not know if or when she will return. Perhaps I will have to wait until we are reunited in the earth, but as I stumble toward the cottage, a lone starling sings from the bough of the holly.

Acknowledgements

It's not until you stop and think about it that you realize how many people help you on your writing journey. Sometimes it's the big things, like beta-reading and cover design, and sometimes it's the little things, such as kind words from friends that banish the clouds.

I would like to thank my husband, Tony, for his never ending encouragement, for creating an incredible book trailer, and for helping me find my way through the maze of glazing and pottery techniques. You may not have the studio you once dreamed of, but the ceramics part of your degree has been put to good use here.

To my late mother, who inspired a love of story-telling in me from the start, and my sweet, old dad who believes in everything I do. Love eternal.

To Samantha Kolesnik, who has turned a dream of seeing my longer fiction published into a reality. I will be eternally grateful. May you and Off Limits Press go from strength to strength!

To my editor, Karmen Wells, for casting her discerning gaze over this manuscript. I learned so much from you in the process. Thank you.

To fellow Off Limits authors: Laurel, Tim, Hailey, you have welcomed me with open arms and so many words of encouragement. I am truly grateful.

My Twitter friends, of whom there are too many to mention by name, thank you so much for your positivity and endless banter. You keep me motivated when times are tough, and I appreciate each and every one of you far more than you know.

Last but not least, to my readers and reviewers. You give purpose to what can be a lonely task.

Biography

Catherine McCarthy is a spinner of dark tales from Wales, U.K.

She writes horror with heart and has recently published a new collection of short stories, Mists and Megaliths. The collection is set in Wales and includes classic ghost stories, cosmic horror, eco-horror, and even a dark comedy in a modern setting.

Her short stories and flash fiction have been published in various places online and in anthologies, including those by The BFS, Crystal Lake Publishing, Flame Tree Press, Curiosities, and Kandisha Press.

When she is not writing, she may be found walking the Welsh coast path or lurking in ancient graveyards reading Machen or Poe.

Discover more at:
https://www.catherine-mccarthy-author.com/

CPSIA information can be obtained
at www.ICGtesting.com
Printed in the USA
BVHW030640240422
635193BV00001B/12

9 781737 463306